Z ANE PRESENTS

THE *Reunion* SHOW

HELL HOUSE 3

REALITY TV DRAMA

Dear Reader:

In Brenda Hampton's *Hell House*, she introduced us to six unique characters from some of her bestselling novels, placed them into a house and let the drama begin. Now in the finale of the trilogy, we discover who is the last person standing and who is $100,000 richer.

Reality television in novel form was a clever concept as Brenda selected specific characters for her hell house setting.

And these roommates in an extremely tight living space definitely bring commotion as they vie for the monetary prize.

If you didn't catch the first title in the series, you may pick up a copy and follow up with book two, *The Roof is On Fire*. You'll have the opportunity to see how it all started.

As always, thanks for supporting the authors of Strebor Books. We always try to bring you groundbreaking, innovative stories that will entertain and enlighten. I can be located at www.facebook.com/AuthorZane or reached via email at Zane@eroticanoir.com.

Blessings,

Zane

Publisher
Strebor Books
www.simonandschuster.com

ZANE PRESENTS

THE

Reunion

HELL HOUSE 3

SHOW

REALITY TV DRAMA

BRENDA HAMPTON

STREBOR BOOKS

NEW YORK LONDON TORONTO SYDNEY

Strebor Books
P.O. Box 6505
Largo, MD 20792
http://www.streborbooks.com

ISBN 978-1-59309-540-6
ISBN 978-1-4767-4620-3 (ebook)
LCCN 2014931229

First Strebor Books trade paperback edition September 2014

Cover design: www.mariondesigns.com
Cover photograph: © Keith Saunders/Keith Saunders Photos

10 9 8 7 6 5 4 3 2 1

Manufactured in the United States of America

For information regarding special discounts for bulk purchases, please contact Simon & Schuster Special Sales at 1-866-506-1949 or business@simonandschuster.com

The Simon & Schuster Speakers Bureau can bring authors to your live event. For more information or to book an event, contact the Simon & Schuster Speakers Bureau at 1-866-248-3049 or visit our website at www.simonspeakers.com.

Hell House was down to three people who had something to prove. Sylvia had been voted out of the house because of her fakeness, Prince had been kicked out for fighting, and Chase had walked out on her own free will. She'd gotten what she needed—sex.

My fate was now in the hands of Jada and Roc, only because Jeff felt as if I had broken the rules when I invited Brashaney to come inside. I couldn't believe this bullshit. If he ordered me to leave, I had already concocted another plan for my unfortunate situation.

I narrowed my eyes and moistened my dry lips with my tongue as I waited to hear Jada and Roc's verdict on me leaving the house. Jada made a ticking sound with her mouth. She searched me from head to toe while scratching her head.

"Dang, Jaylin, I don't know what to do. I hate to be put into a preditment like this. We have had so much fun around here, haven't we?"

"A lot of fun, and we've learned some valuable things that we need to apply to our everyday lives. The word, however, is *predicament*, not preditment."

She shot me a dirty look. "Thank you for that tad bit of information, but at a time like this, I preferred for you not to go there. Boo, you think my decision shouldn't be hard, but it is. While you know I ain't got nothin' but love for you, this is a challenge that I really and truly want to win. As only you know, we got this li'l thang goin' on between us, and I'm not sure if you gon' follow through." She paused and continued in thought.

I assumed she was thinking about the money I had offered her. She could forget it if she made the decision to throw me out over some bullshit.

"Okay," she said, smacking. "What I'm hopin' is that you're a man of your word like you say you are. And that you'll be happy for me if I win." She paused to touch her chest. "With all of that bein' said, my dear, sweet, loveable friend, I've enjoyed your company soooo much, and I don't know what I'mma do without you around here. But you did break the rules. Therefore, you need to go pack yo bags and get yo highly-educated self out of here."

I almost couldn't believe her decision. Then again, yes I could. I said not one word. Nothing but silence soaked the room as I looked over her shoulder at Roc. The ball was in his court. He damn sure better know how to play it. If not, he was going to be fucked!

Roc smirked and massaged his hands together. He licked his lips, and without giving it much more thought, hopped up from his seat and came over to me. I suspected how this was going to turn out, especially by the smirk on his face.

"Peace, bro, you got to go." He saluted me and then turned to Jeff. "The rules must be followed. This is what happens when you play by your own rules."

Jeff looked at me with glee in his eyes. I guess he thought I was going to act a fool and get my clown on, but I surprised everyone when I stood and casually walked over to Jada.

"Give me a hug," I said, opening my arms.

At first, she hesitated but then she stood to embrace me. "You ain't mad at me, are you?" she asked.

"Not at all. This is a challenge and everybody must play to win."

I let go of her and then turned to Roc. I slapped my hand against his, but I didn't say one word. I did, however, have more to say to Jeff. I asked him to meet me in the backyard, so no one could hear our conversation.

"What's up, Jaylin?" he asked. "What's on your mind?"

"A whole lot. For starters, I'mma need for you to come clean about some things."

"Things like what? What are you referring to?"

This was total speculation on my part, but I went for it. I figured that Jeff was somehow or someway involved in what was transpiring behind the scenes, even though I didn't know the exact details.

"I'm referring to a flash drive that shows some sexual activities taking place in this house. That flash drive was in the hands of someone who shouldn't have had it. I question who gave it to her. My answer would be you or Chase. I also know there are some pictures floating around here that shouldn't be. And to be honest with you, Jada told me some things in private that maybe she should've have said. So, I know more than you think I know. And from what I do know, it's enough to shut down Hell House right now."

I lied my ass off, but he seemed nervous enough to let me know that he was in on something. Plus, he hadn't denied anything yet, so I figured I was on to something.

I poked at his chest with my finger. "Here's what you need to know. And once I'm done telling you, you can sigh from relief and wipe some of the sweat from your forehead. The specific de-tails of what is transpiring between you and the ladies, I don't want to know about it. As long as it doesn't involve me, I'm good. I'm already on my way out, but here's the deal. If I'm being asked to leave, then there needs to be a legitimate reason for me to exit. You know that bullshit with Brashaney was a setup, and I know it, too. So, I'm going to stay here for one more night and invite the woman of my choice over here. Then there will be no questions about me breaking the rules. There will be no hard feelings, and by tomorrow afternoon, I'll be out of here and out of your way."

He pondered for a while, figuring that I had the capability of causing this whole thing to come crashing down. He certainly didn't want that to happen, so he slowly nodded.

"Tomorrow. No more delays, Jaylin, I want you to leave. I don't want you to discuss anything with Roc or Jada about your assump-tions, and believe me when I say you don't have all of the facts."

"I repeat…I don't care about the facts. As long as they don't involve me. So, do we have a deal or not?"

"Deal," Jeff said, nodding. "Now, I'm going back inside to tell Jada and Roc that you'll be leaving tomorrow. I don't know how they'll feel about it, but again, I need for you to keep quiet about my involvement in any of this."

"My lips are sealed. Before we go back inside, though, I'll need my phone. I'm sure that since you suspected I'd be leaving today, you have it on you."

He reached into his pocket and tossed my cell phone to me. Afterward, we went back inside. Jada and Roc were sitting on the couch laughing and talking. Jeff cleared his throat and scratched his head.

"Instead of leaving right away, Jaylin will be leaving by tomorrow afternoon. After a long discussion, and because I'm not completely convinced that he invited Brashaney into this house, I'm allowing him to stay for one more day. After that, he's out and the two of you can start doing whatever you guys need to do to win this challenge."

"You mean to tell me that we gotta stay one more day in this house with that fool?" Jada spoke in a joking manner. "I guess that's okay. It ain't no big deal."

"I'm good, too." Roc stood and stretched. "Tomorrow it is."

"Thank you both for understanding," Jeff said. "This was an unfortunate situation, but I'm glad that we're on the same page and that everything got resolved." He turned to me. "Jaylin, I'll see you tomorrow. Don't forget what we discussed."

I didn't bother to reply. He jetted and Roc walked off to the bedroom. Jada remained on the couch. Her eyes bugged when she saw me pull out my cell phone to use it.

"Uh, excuse me. What are you doin'? You ain't supposed to be usin' that phone."

I relaxed on the couch and punched in my four-digit code to listen to my messages. "Mind your business. Just in case you forgot, I don't have to play by the rules anymore. This challenge is over for me. You voted to throw me out of here, remember?"

She pouted and sat silently. I had several messages, but the most recent one was from Chase. How she'd gotten my cell phone number, I didn't know.

Jaylin Rogers, where have you been all of my life? I'm sitting here in the privacy of my home, sipping on wine, watching TV, and thinking about you. I have no idea how much longer you're going to be in that stupid house, but whenever you embark upon some free time, why don't you make it your business to come see me.

She left her address and phone number for me to contact her. I stroked the hair on my chin, contemplating if I should make that move or not. The more I thought about it, it didn't seem like a bad move to make, considering Jeff's change of heart. I wanted additional details about what was going on around here.

Jada was paying close attention to me, but I ignored her and made another call. When she heard me say Nokea's name, she slapped her leg and laughed.

"Oooo, is that Nokea? If so, let me talk to her. I got a few things that I need to tell her. Does she have any idea what you've been doing up in here? I'm sure you won't be tellin' her what went down, but then again, she probably already knows you a ho'."

I turned my back to her and continued my conversation with Nokea. "I'll be home tomorrow. Kiss my babies for me and tell them I'll see them soon."

"I'm sure they'll be happy to hear that," Nokea said. "I'm sorry you didn't win, but I'm glad you'll be coming home. It hasn't been the same without you."

I didn't bother to reply. I preferred to keep my conversation short with Nokea. She knew I was still on edge about her relationship with Tyrese. I told her I would holler later, and instead of contacting my best friend, Shane, I decided to wait until tomorrow. I was sure he would have plenty of questions about why I didn't win. I didn't feel like answering them, even though I was really the big winner in all of this.

To relax for a minute, I laid my cell phone on the table and placed my hands behind my head. I propped my feet on the table and stared at the TV. Jada was trying to distract me with her puzzling looks.

"I'm glad you're stayin' here for one more night," she whispered and then looked over her shoulder. "I don't know what I'm gon' do around here with Roc's ol' borin' self, and I'm sholl gon' miss you."

I nodded and straightened my trimmed goatee with the tips of my fingers. "Jada, just so you know, I'm not giving you one penny. If you win this challenge, and I suspect that you will, it won't be because you played fair and square. It's obvious that you've been doing some sneaky shit."

She opened her mouth wide, as if she were shocked by my accusation.

From a distance, I looked inside of her mouth. "I didn't know your mouth could get that wide. Is it stuck or what?"

"You darn right it is. How dare you claim to be a man of your word and then renigga on givin' me the money? I am gon' to win this challenge fair and square, so you will have to pay up."

"Renege or renigga? Whatever renigga means, I'm not paying you anything."

"It means that you done made a nigga move by tryin' to run and not pay up. Boy, I tell you, some men ain't shit."

I couldn't believe she was actually sitting there upset with me. Other than Jeff, I wanted no one to know that I had the flash drive. It took everything that I had not to tell Jada, but she kept going on and on about the deal I *renigged* on. I was forced to silence her. I removed the flash drive from my pocket and waved it in front of her eyes.

"Weren't you looking for this?"

Her mouth clamped shut. She scratched between her thick cornrows that were braided straight back.

"Yeah, that's what I thought," I said. "I suspect that Chase knows something about this too, and if I wanted to end this today, I could. But I'm not going to because it doesn't seem to be in my best interest. So for the record, you fucked up our deal with the money thing, not me."

She reached out to snatch the flash drive, but I was too quick for her. I put it back into my pocket. There was no way she was getting it.

"Okay then, keep the darn thing. I don't care. It ain't nothin' important on there anyway."

"Important? No. Damaging? Yes. Chase may be more familiar with what I'm talking about. Maybe I should give her a call, so we can discuss what's on the flash drive."

I reached for my cell phone and punched in Chase's number. Jada sat speechless. That let me know that she was concerned about what Chase would say. After a few rings, she answered.

"This is Jaylin," I announced. "I got your message, and it was good hearing from you. The purpose for my call is to invite you to come see me tonight."

"Where are you? At home?"

"No, I'm still at Hell House. I'll be leaving tomorrow, but I need to get at you about a few things. Can you make it here within the hour?"

She paused for a few seconds before answering. "Maybe within a couple of hours or so I can. I was in the middle of something. But before I make any moves, tell me what this is about."

"It's about us. I wanted to see you again. You rushed out of here so quickly that I didn't get a chance to say goodbye like I wanted to."

She hesitated again, but finally said she would come.

"That's what's up," I said, winking at Jada. "Holla soon."

She shook her head. "Why are you invitin' that heifer back into this house? You breakin' all the rules. Does Jeff approve of you doin' all of this?"

"I can do whatever I want to around here. Don't concern yourself with me. I'm curious as to why you're poking your nose in my business, especially when you should be out there partying with Roc. He's chilling by the pool, and I'm sure he may want your company."

She rolled her eyes and threw her hand back. "Forget Roc. I want to know what you're up to."

"No more than what you've been up to. As a reminder to you, in case you forgot, we're all being watched. Be careful who you trust, all right? Don't say that I didn't warn you. I just did."

I stood and left the living room, leaving Jada confused and in deep thought like I wanted her to be.

Chase

I thought I was done with Hell House. At least until the reunion show. But Jaylin's phone call surprised me, especially since he'd invited me to come back to the house. Jeff had already called to give me the scoop on their conversation. I needed to find out exactly what Jaylin knew or what he didn't know. I assumed it wasn't much, but he told Jeff that Jada had been running her big mouth. I couldn't wait to see her and give her a piece of my mind for telling Jaylin what was up.

It was almost 10:00 PM. I knocked on the door to Hell House and was glad to see Jada's wideness through the glass door. She opened it for me to come inside. While standing in the foyer, I wasted no time telling her how I felt about her snitching.

"You fucked up, Jada. I can't believe you betrayed me. And I thought you were eager to win this challenge and put some money into your pockets?"

"I am, but you need to correct your tone and tell me what the hell you're talking about."

"Don't play stupid. This could be a major setback for us. If you've been in here running your mouth to Jaylin, I'm so done with you. Please tell me how in the hell did he get that flash drive? A little birdie told me that he has it, so don't lie. The question is why did you give it to him?"

Jada frowned and rolled her neck around. "To hell with you and your little birdie who goes by the name of Jeff. He don't know what the hell he's talkin' about, and neither do you. I haven't said nothin' to Jaylin. If he told anybody that I have, he's a liar. If he knows anything, he got his information from Jeff, not me. As for the flash drive, I had it hidden in the closet. Jaylin must've found it. I don't know how, because it was hidden away in my shoe. Or maybe it was still in my pocket."

"Hidden, but certainly not hidden good enough," Jaylin said from behind us.

Jada and I snapped our heads to the side. I wondered if he'd heard everything I'd said. At this point, I wasn't going to say another word until I found out what was really going on.

"We're done with this conversation right now," I said to Jada. "But we will definitely talk more about it later."

I turned to Jaylin, forcing a smile. The sight of him was very pleasing to the eyes, but I was a little nervous about our meeting. I hoped he wouldn't notice.

"Now that I'm here," I said, sauntering toward him. "Did you miss me? Or should I ask, what exactly are you going to do with me?"

"No, can't say that I've missed you, but I'm glad you came. Follow me, so we can catch up on a few things. And before I forget, welcome back."

I followed behind him. Jada followed behind me, damn near walking on the back of my heels. She tapped my shoulder and I quickly swung around.

"Don't tell him nothin'," she whispered. "He's playin' on yo intellagant. Trust me when I say he is."

Unfortunately, she didn't understand how worried I was. The issues with her vocabulary worked me even more. Her opinion didn't even matter to me because she wasn't *intelligent* enough to form one that made sense. I rolled my eyes and kept it moving.

"Screw you then, heifer," she said loud enough for Jaylin to turn around. "That's why you got a piece of meat stuck between your teeth. Those tight-ass jeans gon' give you a nasty yeast infection, and I hope you fall and bust yo big head with those ugly, cheap heels you got on. I saw those at Big Lots, so don't be up in here like you got Saks Fifth Avenue taste when you don't."

I had to silence her so she'd stop embarrassing herself and me.

"Jada, please go somewhere and take your meds. You are really tripping. I seriously wonder what has gotten into you."

"When the two of y'all get done exchanging jabs," Jaylin said, "I'll be in the game room. Chase, don't have me waiting too long, all right?"

He walked off, leaving me in thought about what a real jerk he was. For now, though, I was fuming behind Jada's actions. I had to address her right away. I wanted to cuss her out, but instead, I did my best to bring this psycho bitch back to reality and on my side.

"You're pissing me off, Jada. I'm curious about what has gotten into you, but no matter what it is, we're too close to getting this over and done with. All of this arguing and disrespect needs to end. I don't know what I did to upset you. Whatever it is, would you please tell me?"

She shot me a dirty look and hissed. "Bitch, you accused me of doin' somethin' that I didn't do. You're makin' me uncomfortable by comin' here to be with Jaylin. I don't know what the hell is goin' on with y'all, and I ain't nobody's fool. All I know is y'all could be tryin' to trick me. If that's the case, you'd better think twice before you think about stabbin' me in the back."

She was a pain in the ass. I tried to convince her that what she was referring to wasn't the case, or I hoped it wouldn't be.

"I wouldn't backstab you, okay? It's too late in the game to change the plan, and I'm sticking with you because I trust you. All I'm asking is that you trust me on this. I'm not trying to do anything with Jaylin but pump information from him. Jeff requested it, so that's why I'm here."

She pursed her lips. "Chile, please. You're not goin' to be able to pump no information from him by riding his dick, so stay away from it. I'mma let you do you, but just so you know, I will be keepin' my eyes on both of y'all."

"Good. Watch all you want. Maybe you'll learn something about getting a man to do exactly what you want him to do."

I winked at Jada and walked off. As soon as I stepped in the backyard, I spotted Roc sitting by the pool, listening to music. I said hello to him, but all he did was suck his teeth and turn his head to avoid me. I was surprised by his actions, so I went up to him.

"It's like that, huh? Are you that upset with me for leaving you? If so, don't worry. You'll be seeing much more of me in the weeks to come."

"Bitch, get the fuck away from me before I get up and slap the shit out of you."

My eyes grew wide from his bluntness. I let out a soft snicker and shrugged. "Wow. I didn't know it was that serious. Since you're so bitter, I'll mosey on into the game room with Jaylin and go where the real fun is at."

Roc didn't respond. He bobbed his head to the rap music he was listening to and closed his eyes. I walked away, thinking about my future plans to make his life a living hell. I couldn't help but to smile.

I entered the game room, seeing that Jaylin had already prepared drinks for us. I fanned my hand in front of my face.

"It's awfully hot out there," I said in a teasing manner. "Roc and

Jada seem real tense, but here you are in here with a smile on your face, making drinks. You're the one going home tomorrow, so why are you so thrilled?"

"Because, at the end of the day, I still consider myself a winner." Jaylin handed me a glass with alcohol in it. "I assume you will be too, but that's just my opinion."

I took the glass from his hand and clinked my glass against his. "I'll drink to that. Winning is my motto."

He drank from his glass and I tackled mine. When he took a seat at the bar, I sat next to him.

"So, what's on your mind?" I asked. "I'm sure you didn't invite me here so you could admire my beauty did you?"

A grin appeared on his face. "Of course not. But I did invite you here so that we could have a down-to-earth, truthful talk. In my heart, I believe that you've been up to no good. I hoped that you'd be willing to provide some specific details about your plan, or of a plan that Jeff has been plotting all along. Somehow, Jada is involved and it appears that Roc and I are the targets."

"Hmmm, seems like you've been doing a little homework, but not much. Besides, what makes you think that I would tell you anything, if what you're assuming is correct?"

"Because I know how much you like me. Thing is, I like you too. I think we may be on to something special, and I don't think that the connection we made should end here. Ya feel me?"

I leaned in closer to him, speaking in a whisper. "Oh, I feel you, and I would definitely love to feel you again. I'm down with building new friendships, but only ones that can last more than one night. The question is do you feel me?"

"Whether it lasts one night, one year, or ten years is totally up to you. Most women that I know can't stand to be around me for that long, so be careful what you wish for. But let's start today as being friends. As my new friend, you can start from the beginning and tell me everything you know."

I smiled and picked up my glass to take a sip. Jaylin didn't think I'd be foolish enough to tell him everything I'd been up to, did he? Shame on him for underestimating me. There was no question that he had an effect on me, but no man would ever make a fool out of me.

I stood and removed the short jacket I wore. It covered my yellow tank shirt that squeezed my breasts together. Jaylin's eyes traveled directly to them.

"I'll tell you what, Jaylin. Since you don't know as much as I thought you knew, I'll tell you a few things that you want to know, provided that you can beat me at a game of pool. If you lose, then I get to choose the positions you'll put me in tonight, when you'll have the pleasure of fucking me. Bet?"

He didn't immediately respond to my comment, but I noticed a slight nod. Appearing confident that he'd win the game, he stood and rubbed his hands together. "That sounds like a winning proposal, but to make it more fun, how about one missed shot will require us to lose a piece of clothing? And if you miss your shot, I can ask you any question that I want to instead of waiting until the end to ask questions."

"I'm down with that, but I'd better put my jacket back on. With the way I play, I'm sure I'll need it."

The game got underway after Jaylin racked the balls and took the first shot to break them. He directed me to take the next shot, but truthfully, I was no good at playing. Still, I wanted to do my best, so I bent over the table and took the shot. Unfortunately, my ball missed the hole. I snapped my finger. and removed the first piece of clothing, my jeans. My turquoise thong showed, and to put it on display, I sashayed over to a chair, laying my jeans across it.

"Nice thong," he complimented. "But I need to hit you with question number one. Have you conspired with others to win the Hell House challenge?"

He bent over to take his shot.

"Yes, I have conspired with others to win this challenge."

He made the shot, but took off one of his tennis shoes, tossing it over his shoulder.

"Cheater," I said and then winked. All he did was laugh.

I took the next shot, missing that one too. "Damn," I said, snapping my fingers.

I was seriously trying to make the shot, but this time I removed my jacket. He couldn't wait to hit me with the next question.

"Does your plan include Jada and Jeff?"

Without hesitating, I answered. "Yes."

He stroked the hair on his chin, and to no surprise, he made his next shot. Still, he removed his other tennis shoe, obviously not playing by the rules.

It was my turn again. The next three shots that I took, I missed. I was now down to only my thong. With him making all of his shots, he was in his red Calvin Klein boxers and a wife beater.

He asked the next question. "Will any of your plans affect me?"

"No."

"Are you seeking revenge against Roc?"

"Yes."

"Why?"

I put chalk on the end of my stick and had no problem answering his question. I faced him with my firm breasts standing at attention. My nipples were hard from glaring at the growth of his muscle.

"Here's the deal," I said. "Jada and I are going to win the challenge because we have enough damaging information against Roc that will send him packing and flying out of the door. You have nothing, whatsoever, to do with this, and I know for a fact that you could not care less about the money. Jada and I need it way more than you do, so allow us to do what we must to cross the finish line."

Without responding, Jaylin took his next shot, and then I took mine. This time, I made it.

"Nice shot, nice ass, and beautiful titties," Jaylin complimented. "You're right. I couldn't care less about the money, but I do believe in playing fair. Roc will be blindsided by all of this. Explain to me why you are coming down so hard on the brotha?"

"It's personal. If I told you, you wouldn't understand. And the truth of the matter is life isn't fair. We both know that, so don't act like I'm sharing something with you that you don't already know."

"I agree, but I expected more from you, Chase. I didn't think you'd get yourself involved in personal, petty issues that may turn out to backfire. You must know that Roc is nobody's fool."

"I never said he was a fool, but this time he will be my little sucker. Regardless of what you say, he's coming down, because I don't appreciate how he's treated me, and I don't like men who wish to have their cake and eat it too. If you're one of those men, I'm sure you can understand where a woman like me is coming from. So, if I were you, Jaylin Rogers, I wouldn't have too much sympathy for Roc, especially since he didn't hesitate when it came to voting you out of here. I wonder, if the shoe was on the other foot, if he'd be as concerned about you as you seem to be about him?"

"Trust me when I say I'm not as concerned about him as I am about you. I'm trying to prevent you from making a big mistake by interfering in his personal life. The buck should stop here, shouldn't it?"

I shrugged, wholeheartedly disagreeing. "Maybe it should, but that'll be my choice to make. And if you're so concerned about me, I can show you what you should be concerned about more than anything."

I laid my pool stick on the table and climbed on top of it. While on my hands and knees, I crawled to the center of the table and looked to my left at Jaylin.

"This is what you should concern yourself with. Go check things out from the back and see what you can do with it."

He studied my flawless body as he circled the pool table. When he got to my backside, I spread my knees further apart so he could see the string from my thong being swallowed by the folds of my moist pussy lips.

"Get a good look," I invited. "Concern yourself with the over-flowing wetness and let me know what you're prepared to do about it."

He remained at the end of the table, narrowing his eyes. He touched my right ass cheek first and then put his other hand on the left one.

"Do you mind if I get a closer look?" he asked.

"Please do. Help yourself and examine it how you wish."

He spread my cheeks to look deeper inside. I felt the string sink further into my slippery lips. I was so wet from thinking about him being inside of me again.

"Umph, umph, umph," he said. "I must say that things are look-ing pretty damn good from where I see it. But the problem is, in order for me to indulge myself, you need to win this game. If you don't win, I can't fulfill our agreement. It'll be unfortunate if we have to leave here deprived."

"I agree, so I have a better idea. How about I throw in the towel and watch you play the remainder of the game? After you're finished, we'll discuss our little so-called agreement and consider changing the rules. I have a feeling that some adjustments may have to be made."

He removed his hands from my ass cheeks and picked up the pool stick. As I remained on the table, he worked around me and carefully shot his balls, including the eight ball, into the holes. That made him the winner of our game. He acknowledged so when he laid the stick back down on the table. This time, he stood in front of me with his muscle-packed arms folded.

"I win, you lose," he confirmed.

I lay on my stomach and bent my knees. "Lucky you. I didn't think I would win anyway, but I do hope that you'll be willing to reconsider our agreement; after all, we didn't shake on it. In addition to that, you gained a lot of information tonight. I told the truth, and you appreciate my honesty, don't you?"

"I do, and thank you for being honest during our little Q&A session. But here's the deal, baby. You can't change the rules in the middle of the game. You may not play fair, but, I do." Jaylin laid his wife beater on the pool table, right in front of me. "I didn't see any towels, but feel free to use that to wipe the wetness between your legs. A loss is a loss and sex between us will have to take place at another time. Good night, Chase. Like always, it's been a pleasure."

I was almost speechless when he walked away. I yelled after him. He turned at the door.

"There may never be a next time," I said. "It doesn't make sense for you to be hard like that when I'm clearly capable of taking care of that for you."

"A homeless woman with no teeth in her mouth is capable of taking care of my hard-on too. I'm not in the mood tonight, baby, and to be completely honest with you, my dick always gets enthusiastic at times, even when I'm not."

Before I could respond, he walked out the door. I released a deep sigh and rolled my eyes in several directions.

"Bastard," I said underneath my breath.

His arrogance worked the heck out of me, but it was such a turn on too. I got off the table, got dressed, and left the house before Jada or Roc saw me. I didn't want to see them. As mad as I was, saying the wrong thing to me would get them cussed out. Especially Jada.

There was no question that I loved sexy women, but the ones who liked to play seduction games with me wouldn't get too far. Then, it also depended on what kind of mood I was in. Last night, I was in no mood to deal with Chase. The goal was to get as much information that I could from her. Even though I believed she had told me the truth, I still didn't like how any of this was playing out. Then again, it was wise for me to let the chips fall where they may and step back. Sort of like chill and observe things from afar. Then make a move that would blow everyone away. Considering all that I knew about Hell House, I'd say the ball was in my court. Nonetheless, it was almost time for me to go.

Roc hadn't said one word to me. It seemed like he was trying to avoid me. Of course, I wanted to tell the brotha what was lurking in his future, but I'd thought about what Chase had said last night. If the shoe were on the other foot, would he get after me to share what was up? I doubted that he would.

Right after my shower, I put on some clothes and made my way to the kitchen, where I could smell maple syrup. I hadn't been in the kitchen for one minute before Roc picked up his plate, tossed his head back at me and walked outside. Jada, however, stood with a big smile plastered on her face. She had a plate in her hand that was piled high with two Belgian waffles topped with whipped cream and strawberries. Several slices of turkey bacon were on the plate, along with scrambled eggs.

"Here you go, sweetie," she said. "I couldn't let you leave here with an empty stomach."

I walked up to her and looked at the food. "Thanks, but you didn't put any poison in it, did you?"

Her face fell flat. "Fuck you, Jaylin. I call myself bein' nice to you, but you always gotta go there with somethin' stupid."

I removed the plate from her hand and thanked her again. "I really do appreciate this, but let me remind you again. I'm still not giving the money to you."

I walked over to the kitchen table and took a seat. Jada followed me. She bent over, put her elbows on the table, and pressed her hands against her cheeks.

"Please," she begged. "You got a heart in there somewhere, Jaylin, and you can't be mad at me for makin' you leave. You know I had to vote you out of here so I could win this challenge."

"Yes, I can be mad at you. If I can eat this bullshit that you cooked for me this morning, then I can do anything I want to, can't I?"

She opened her mouth wide and blew her hot breath in my face. "Cool off, fool. You're too hot this mornin' and I'm tryin' to be nice. If you don't like the food, I will be happy to go to the fridge and retrieve an apple for you."

"Retrieve? Look at you trying to use a *big* word and pronounce it correctly. I'm proud of you, baby. Real proud."

"Great. And when I put my tidday in your mouth to shut you up, I hope you'll be proud of that too."

Annoying me, she blew her breath on me again. I cocked my head back to give us some space.

"Seriously, you should've brushed your teeth this morning. It's apparent that you didn't. And even though the food looks good, why put all this whipped cream on top of the waffles? All you're doing is adding too much sugar, when the strawberries are enough."

She rushed over to the fridge to get the container of whipped cream. "I knew you were goin' to complain about the whipped cream, but let me show you a little somethin' about food that you don't know. Bay-bee, there are only fifteen calories in that whipped cream and one gram of fat. The sugar content is less than one gram, so what do you have to say about that?"

I removed the whipped cream from the waffles. "I say that you're easily misled and you need to check the servings, per container. What you mentioned only accounts for two tablespoons. You have at least twenty or thirty tablespoons piled on my waffles. Sell that shit to somebody else, not me."

Jada rolled her eyes and snatched my plate. "Ugh," she said. "You think you know it all, don't you? I swear you get on my nerves and—"

I rushed behind her and snatched a piece of turkey bacon off the plate before she tossed it in the trash.

"The waffles were soggy, but the bacon is good," I said, chewing fast to irritate her.

She playfully pushed my shoulder and then got me an apple from the fridge, tossing the fruit to me.

"Thanks," I said. "This is much better."

"I hope so." Jada walked up to me, as I stood by the counter. "So, tell me what you and Chase talked about last night. She didn't leave here until real late, and I saw her ass hiked up on that pool table. I bet she had that whole room smellin' like tilapia, didn't she? She is so nasty to me, and that pussy of hers is tired of that bitch tryin' to use it to her advantage."

I bit into the apple, shaking my head at Jada.

"You know she's foul," Jada continued. "And if she don't smell like tilapia, you be smellin' like it 'cause I believe you get mo' pussy than ten NBA players put together, don't you? Chase was throwin' that cat at you last night, and when I saw you walk off, I was like… hell, nah! I cracked up and ran to hide behind one of those chairs. You didn't see me, though. I was hidin' real good."

"Actually, you weren't. I saw you peeking into the game room, and I also saw you trying to hide behind the chair. Next time, choose somewhere else. Behind one of those bushes outside may have been better."

Her brows shot up. "Did you just try to insult me by implyin' that I was too wide and the chair couldn't hide me? Is that what you're sayin'?"

"What I'm saying is behind a chair ain't a good place to hide. Now, it's been real, baby. I need to start packing so I can get out of here. Are we done?"

She lowered her head, pouted, and displayed fake sadness. "I guess. Don't let me hold you up any longer." She threw her arms around me, giving me a hug. As she squeezed my ass, I gave hers a pat.

"See you at the reunion show," I said. "Be good, and remember to watch your back."

As soon as those words left my mouth, Jeff came in carrying groceries. A fake smile covered his face as he saw Jada and me embracing.

"Jaylin, what time shall I call a cab for you? Are you already packed?" he asked.

"I'm getting to it right now, but I don't do cabs. I'll call someone to come get me."

I walked away and went into the bedroom to call Shane.

"If you're calling me," he said, "I take it that you didn't win."

"I can't win them all, but don't count me out just yet. I need for you to come pick me up as quickly as you can. Can you handle that for me?"

"Within the next hour or so, I can. Be ready when I get there. I can't wait to tell you about all the shit that's been happening while you were away on your little adventure."

"You know I'm not up to hearing about that break-up, make-up shit between you and Tiffanie. My only question is were you capable of increasing the digits in my bank account? That's all I want to know."

"The love for money always motivates me, so you can be sure that your account is in better standings. See you in a bit, but prepare yourself for relationship drama that doesn't solely revolve around me."

I didn't bother to question him because everyone already knew that drama was in conjunction with my middle name. I told him I'd see him soon and then ended the call. Afterward, I took my time packing, and one by one, I carried my luggage to the front door. I wasn't sure where Roc was, but Jada was now in the kitchen eating ice cream. While licking the spoon, she kept taking peeks at me.

"Do you need some help?" she yelled from afar and laughed. "If so, I'm sure Roc will help you."

I ignored her. When Shane arrived, I carried my luggage to the trunk of his car. He helped me put the luggage inside while Jada stood in the doorway, watching.

"Lord have mercy! Is that yo friend?" she shouted.

I didn't bother to respond, neither did Shane. We got in the car, but the moment he got ready to pull off, Jada rushed outside, waving her hands in the air as if I'd forgotten something.

"Wha…wait a minute." She bent down, huffing and puffing like she was out of breath. Shane lowered the window and she looked past him to talk to me. "Don't hurt yourself watchin' what's on that flash drive, Jaylin, and when you see Roc's loooong penis emerge from his sweatpants, don't get jealous." She winked and then shifted her eyes to Shane. Her smile got wider and she batted her lashes. "Meanwhile, my name is Jada. I'm the dick-less chick in the house, and everybody done got hooked up except for me. Is there any chance that if I give you my phone number, the two of us can hook up?"

Shane lifted his hand to show her the ring on his finger. "Sorry, sweetheart, I'm taken," he said. "I don't think my wife would approve."

She stood up straight with her lips pursed. "Y'all men be killin' me with that mess. I bet yo thang drippin' right now from the juices of another woman. Stop playin' so doggone much about being taken. If I was a skinny bitch with curves, the only place you'd be takin' me is to your bedroom." Shane's face twisted. He appeared taken aback by Jada's comment. She continued to rant. "Sittin' in the driver's seat with a head full of dreads like you all that. Negro, please."

"Just drive off," I said to Shane. "I'll explain Miss Jada Mahoney to you later."

Shane took his eyes off Jada to put the car in reverse. "I can't wait to hear all about it. It sounds as if you may have had yourself a good time."

I laid the seat back, put my hands behind my head, and closed my eyes. "A damn good time," I confirmed. "And I'm looking forward to when we all meet again."

Roc

Seeing Chase back in this house had me hot. I don't know why I let that trick get to me. There was something about her that irked the fuck out of me. It was rare that I felt so much hatred inside for a woman.

As for Jaylin, I was glad that he was gone. I didn't say much to him because there really wasn't much else for me to say. On a for real tip, this was a game—one that I played to win. There was never any love for the next man, but there was some respect. Jeff provided an easy opportunity for Jaylin to exit the house. I would have been a fool for not jumping on it. Now, it was down to Jada and me. There wasn't a chance in hell that she was going to win this challenge. The smart thing for her to do was to pack up her bags and flee. I wanted to tell her that she had no chance at winning this challenge, but I decided to play this thing out, in hopes that we would be going home soon.

I was feeling hyped about going home. I didn't realize how difficult being away from Desa Rae, my kids, and from the fellas who worked at my shop, would be. Being here was starting to feel like torture, and it wasn't like Jada would be able to entertain me for long. I was in deep thought while chilling by myself near the pool, thinking about my mistakes.

Minutes later, Jada came outside to chill with me. She didn't appear to be as giddy as she had been before, maybe because she felt bad for voting Jaylin out of the house.

"Looks like it's just you and me now," she said sadly, sitting next to me in a lounge chair. "What are we gon' do to keep ourselves busy?"

"I say make the best of it, ma. Keep doin' what we've been doin'. I doubt that we'll be here much longer, and I'm curious about how this gon' end."

Jada leaned back and put her ashy feet on the table. She had on thong sandals that didn't make her feet look pretty at all.

"I sholl do need a pedicure. The first place I'm goin' when I leave here is to see that Chinese lady on Chambers Road. She be workin' the heck out of my feet, and the only thing I'm curious about is how she gon' get all this crust to come off. That stuff done built up. See."

Her feet looked like she'd been dancing in a mountain of flour. The cure was lotion. She knew it and I knew it too.

"I already know who gon' win this challenge," she said. "And too bad you gon' be walkin' out of here with your head slumped down."

"Don't play yourself. You know I'm not goin' out like that, so don't count your chickens before they hatch."

"I'm not countin' chickens, but I will be countin' money. That's all I'm gon' say. Until then, I'mma go fix us somethin' to eat. Since Mr. Merry Maids is gone, we gon' have to keep this place clean. Do you mind straightenin' the TV room, takin' out the trash, and cleanin' the bathrooms?"

"I don't mind." I stood to stretch. "But what are you cookin' for us?"

"I'm not sure yet. Jeff brought some goodies earlier today and put them in the fridge. I may fry some chicken and be done with it."

I nodded, and five minutes later, I cranked up the music in the house and we got busy. After I was done straightening the living room, I plopped down the couch and lit a joint. One puff in, Jada rushed over to join me.

"I need a li'l somethin' to get me goin' too." She giggled. "And I feels real bad about my buddy, Jaylin, bein' gone. I miss him already."

I didn't bother to comment. Like me, Jada wanted to win. She didn't give a fuck about Jaylin. If she had, he would still be here. Her move showed me how cutthroat she could be.

She bobbed her head to rapper 2 Chainz's, "I'm Different".

"Yeah, baby, that's what I am," she said with the joint dangling from the corner of her mouth. She snapped her fingers in the air. "This…this weed knows it is fire. How much more do you got?"

She took a long drag then passed the joint back to me.

"I told you before not much, but I'mma need to hit up Prince's neck in the hoods when I get out of here."

"Be sure to let me know. It ain't like I'm gon' say anything to that punk, but you can hook me up on the side."

"You know I will. But you and Prince should let bygones be bygones. You were kind of hard on him, and I still don't know what you had against that brotha."

Her face fell flat and she barked at me. "How about that nigga *beat my ass*. That's what I have against him. I should reach over there to smack you for soundin' so stupid. I wasn't hard on his disrespectful self. I don't like no man who is out of control and sneaky. Besides that, every time he came out of the bathroom, he always walked like he had shit stacked in his ass. It was painful to watch him stride around here like everything was all good."

She frowned, but I cracked up. Since she was in a talkative mood, I switched the subject to Chase.

"So, tell me," I said, licking my thick lips. "What was Chase doin' here last night?"

She shrugged. "I guess she came to get her fuck on, but her plans fell through. Jaylin wasn't havin' it. He was like…like bye bitch, I'm out. I mean, he ran from that corrupt pussy. "

"Smart man, but what did she tell you about me and Jaylin? I get a feelin' that she's up to somethin'."

She jumped up from the couch and sniffed the air. "Daaang. Do you smell that?"

"Smell what? Weed?"

"Nope. Seasoned fried chicken that I must get back to. As for Chase, all I can tell you is what she told me about y'all sex-wise. She said that both of y'all had crooked dicks that hurt like hell. That's it."

She walked off, laughing. I knew how to pump more information from her, but like Jaylin, I was confused by the crooked dick assumption.

"What's with the crooked dick thing?" I made my way into the kitchen where Jada was. She turned down the burner on the stove to slow cook the chicken that was already looking crispy.

"I gotta make sure the inside is done," she said, referring to the chicken. "I definitely don't want to serve you no uncooked chicken, but uh, as far as the crooked dick thingy, you have to ask Chase about that. From what I saw, and have seen, you do have a crooked dick."

"No, I really don't. And I don't believe Chase told you that bull-shit."

She shrugged. "You asked and I told you. You don't have to believe me, but whether she said it or not, your dick is crooked."

There was a smirk on my face; I knew where Jada was going with this. "I know what you're up to, ma. You want me to pull my dick out and prove it to you, don't you?"

She threw her hand back. "Boy, please. You don't have to prove nothin' to me, especially when I already know the real deal."

Just for the hell of it, I lowered my swim trunks and exposed my package to Jada. She had the audacity to squint, as if my dick was too little for her to see.

"Now that you've seen it, where is it crooked at?"

She widened her eyes and then blinked. "It's too limp right now, so I can't tell. Once it gets hard, I'll show you how crooked it is."

I looked down at my meat that was sitting pretty on my sacks. It wasn't hard, but Jada had to do a li'l somethin'-somethin' if she wanted it to grow in her direction.

"I doubt that it will get hard with you standin' there lookin' at it. And I'm not gon' start strokin' it myself."

She licked her lips and kept her eyes locked on it. "I don't think strokin' it would be a good idea, but you can be sure that I would never, ever fall to my knees and put anything like that in my mouth. That thing is too, too thick and my mouth don't stretch that wide."

She stretched her mouth, trying to show me that my dick wouldn't fit. "See," she said. "How in the hell are you holdin' down all of that?"

"Your mouth is waaay too small, but I'll make it work. Meanwhile, we were talkin' about the crooked dick thing." I held my dick in my hand and moved it around so she could observe it. "Feel free to touch it and witness how straight it is. Go ahead and help yourself. You may get a rise out of it."

Jada laughed and tiptoed her way up to me. She poked at my dick with her finger, causing it to bounce on my balls.

"Springy," she said.

"Sometimes."

She lifted it up, causing it to grow, at least a half-inch from the touch of her finger.

"Swelling."

"No doubt."

Jada nodded and then held her hand underneath it, cautiously holding it.

"Heavy."

"Getting heavier."

Another inch was added and Jada's eyes grew wider.

"Oh, shit," she shouted. "Almost there."

"Not hardly."

Jada grinned, and when she wrapped her hand around my package, turning it like a knob, I gave her a few more inches. That was when she snatched her hand away, as if my dick burnt her fingers. She jumped back and held her chest while taking deep breaths.

"Hu...huge!" she shouted. "Damn, Roc! You got one of those Mandingo dicks."

"If you say so, but crooked you do not see."

She slowly moved her head from side to side. "No, it's not crooked. I was gettin' ready to mention Desa Rae's name. If I do, will it grow some more?"

On a for real tip, hearing Desa Rae's name made my steel fall back. I pulled up my swim trunks, figuring that she wouldn't be too happy about me showing what belonged to her to another woman.

"It could have grown some more, but you moved us in the wrong direction. Next time, leave Desa Rae out of the mix."

"Desa Rae or no Desa Rae, you need a license to carry that thing. A woman can kill herself messin' with you. What woman in her right mind would let you put that inside of her? That's one brave bitch. Either Chase is a fool or a damn fool. I know she couldn't hang with that."

My head was swoll. It was always good to hear li'l mamas like Jada give my dick such high praises. "Nah, she couldn't hang, but I know how to work it on certain chicks where it doesn't hurt as much."

She fanned herself with her hand. "In that case, I might be tempted. I hope you take it easy on me. I am gon' get my turn too, right?"

Jada was known for being playful, so I wasn't sure if she was serious or not. I had no intentions to get my freak on with her. What I had done with Chase was already fucking with my head. I didn't need no shit with Jada to add to what I was feeling, so sex between us had to wait for another lifetime. I didn't tell her that, though.

"I'll be real easy on you, ma. Real easy."

She blushed and used a two-prong fork to turn the chicken. Excited, she snapped her fingers to the music that was still playing and swayed her wide hips. Being playful, she bumped her hip with mine and then removed a piece of chicken from the hot grease so I could taste it.

"It's too hot," I said as she put the steamy, greasy chicken up to my mouth. "Wait until it cools off."

"Okay. But go on and get finished cleanin'. By the time you get done with the bathroom, dinner should be ready. I'mma set the table for us and make a pitcher of Kool-Aid."

The least I could do was put the weed bag away and get finished cleaning. Being here with Jada might not be so bad after all. I couldn't think of any other person I would rather be left in Hell House with.

Roc was cool people. Too bad I was going to have to break him
down with the bad news Chase had provided to me. I was worried
about Jaylin sitting on some important information and about
him having the flash drive. Right after dinner with Roc, I snuck
into the bathroom to call Chase. She seemed worried too. She
wasn't happy about our plan being compromised.

I asked if she had told Jaylin anything and she hollered into the
phone. "I didn't tell him no more than you already did."

"Lower your voice, bitch; you're too excited. Don't be mad at
me because he rejected the pussy. That was your fault for tryin' to
throw it at him."

"Screw you, Jada. Your mouth is about to get you dismissed from
the plan. Had he not gotten a hold to that flash drive, we wouldn't
be in this predicament."

She was about to fuck herself. In no way did I like her tone. I
had messed up, but she didn't have to talk to me like I was some
kind of idiot.

"So, I messed up and Jaylin now has the flash drive. Don't think
you can talk to me any kind of way, 'cause the last time I checked,
you walked out of here and left me to handle this. So, cool the
hell out and let me get down like I do. Jaylin won't say anything

to Roc because Jaylin couldn't care less about what happens. That's what he said, so I'mma need for you to have a li'l faith in me workin' this out."

I could hear her sigh over the phone. "I'm trying, but I don't trust Jaylin not to say anything. My suggestion would be for you to hurry up and get this over with. The money is as good as ours if you can convince Roc to leave the house. The information that you have will send him packing. And please do not let him know about Desa Rae and me being sisters. I want to have the pleasure of telling her myself one day."

I only wished that I could be a fly on the wall when that day happened. Chase was scandalous. Roc hadn't a clue about how badly he'd fucked up.

"What we have will make him run out of here. I'm goin' to move quickly on this, just not as quickly as you want me to. I don't get off on hurtin' people as easy as you do, but when money is involved, I gotta do what I must. The next time we talk, I'm confidence this will be over."

"Confident, Jada. The word is *confident*, and I hope you are."

"No, the word is confidence. I have a whole lot of confidence that I can beat yo ass, if you keep on tryin' to tell me how to talk."

I hung up on that heifer. Some people didn't know when to cut it off and keep their mouths shut. I guess Chase didn't realize how much control I had in this matter. It was in her best interest to wise up.

After I flushed the toilet and washed my hands, I felt the cell phone vibrating in my pocket. Chase was never supposed to call me, but I assumed she was upset with me for hanging up on her.

"What is it, Chase?" I snapped.

"Stop with the nonsense, Jada, and let's put the focus back on getting this done. I apologize for raising my voice at you, for accusing you of telling Jaylin certain things, and for correcting your language. But please understand that I'm not happy about Jaylin having that flash drive."

"Like I said, I honestly do not think he cares about none of this. But I'm sure you can read him better than me."

"I would like to think so, but after last night, I'm not so sure. I think he's plotting to do something. That's why we need to hurry this up."

"Maybe he is plotting, but then again, maybe not. After he watches that video on the flash drive, he'll be smilin' his ass off. I watched some of what was on it, and I need to give you a Bad Bitch Award for hangin' with Roc and for leavin' Jaylin after he caressed and massaged all over you like that."

She laughed hysterically. I didn't see anything funny—I was serious.

"I couldn't handle Roc on a good day. There is no secret that he beat me up pretty good. Had me bleeding and everything, but it was nice to have a man inside of me who could fill me up. As for Jaylin, he was exactly what the doctor ordered. Between us, I was a little disappointed about him rejecting me last night. But I assure you that it won't go down like that the next time I see him. Besides, I'm not some airhead chick who thinks pussy is the key to winning his heart. There's so much more to him, and I don't mind taking a little extra time to figure him out."

"Well, if I were in your shoes, I would be head over heels for him and Roc. Earlier, he said I could get it, so I'm curious to see if he was tellin' the truth."

Chase paused for several seconds, before she responded. "No offense, Jada, but I doubt that Roc is interested in you. He's a big flirt who doesn't follow through on what he says. Regardless, you don't have time to pursue sex with him. Stay committed to our mission and save your pursuit of sex for another time."

Yet again, Chase rubbed me the wrong way. If anything, she sounded jealous. "I'm workin' this on my time, not yours. Roc is waitin' for me by the pool, and I have a feelin' that somethin' magical is goin' to happen tonight. I'll keep you informed on how the next several days play out. Bye."

I ended the call and turned off the phone so Chase wouldn't interrupt me again. Unfortunately, though, when I opened the bathroom door, Roc stood on the other side. I wasn't sure if he'd heard all of my conversation or not, but he questioned who I was talking to.

"Sorry about that, but I me…medeate sometimes." Suspicion was clearly in my eyes. "You should've knocked if you needed to use the bathroom."

"I was gettin' ready to, but I didn't because I heard you talkin'. You need to check yourself on that shit, 'cause you was soundin' real coo-coo. And just so you know, ma, the way to pronounce the word is *meditate*, not medeate. Don't get mad at me for correcting you, but what you said didn't make sense."

Everybody correcting me all the time was embarrassing, but Roc had no business going there, especially with his thuggish self. "I get all of that, Roc, and I will try to do better. But since we're on the subject of what do and don't make sense, let me correct you on something. It makes no sense for you to run around here talking about love for yo woman, when you done cracked the code on another bitch's pussy. Not only with yo dick, but also with yo mouth. If you can explain the logic to that, I'd like to hear it. If not, don't worry about me, because my little problem with incorrectly pronouncing words seem minor compared to your problem. Wouldn't you say so?"

He folded his arms across his chest. "The way I see it, I don't have a problem. But if you're hemmed up in the bathroom medeatin', I'd say you do. Now, if you don't mind, I need to take a leak. Any follow up to this conversation will have to wait for another day or time."

I moved out of the way so he could go into the bathroom. Since he didn't say that he'd overheard my conversation with Chase, I assumed he didn't know what was up. Chase was right, though. I had to be more careful before this whole thing blew up in smoke.

When Roc came out of the bathroom, we spent the next few hours hanging out by the pool. It was still kind of early when we hit the sack, and being that we were the only two left, I eased my way in the bed with him. The only thing I had on was a Betty Boop pajama top with no bra or panties. I snuggled close to his bare chest while reading a book to him. Ten minutes in, he interrupted me.

"You know what's strange," he said, clearing his throat. "Desa Rae be readin' to me like this all the time. I think that's real sweet, ma. Continue."

Fuck Desa Rae. I was getting sick of hearing her name, but I pretended that what he said didn't irritate me.

"That's nice, Roc. Now hursh so I can finish gettin' to the good stuff."

I continued on. About fifteen minutes later, I could see his chest heaving in and out. His snores sounded like sizzling bacon frying in grease, and when I looked up, his eyes were closed. Well, I'll be damned. Seeing him in action with Chase and her saying that he wouldn't be interested in me made me curious about sex with him. There was something about him that was so sexy to me, and I loved his tattoos. His black skin was silky smooth; there was no question that he was my kind of man. Make no mistake about it, I wasn't thirsty for no man like Sylvia and Chase. But any woman with her doggone head on straight wouldn't let this opportunity go by.

"Roc," I whispered near his ear. That didn't wake him, so I blew cool air from my breath, over his face. He winced, and with his eyes still closed, he shifted his head to the other side. I touched his smooth, coal-black waves and pressed my lips against his cheek, planting a kiss on it. This time, he squinted to look at me.

"What's up, ma?" he said in a groggy tone.

"What's up is I…I wondered if we could, you know, get a li'l freaky with each other?"

Roc brushed me off. "Go to sleep, Jada. You know we ain't goin' there."

I caught an attitude. "No, I don't know anything except that you told me it was possible. I'm not gon' sweat you, but what's the big deal?"

Now, he was wide awake and had sat up in the bed. Probably because he didn't want me laying on him anymore.

"The big deal is I have a woman. I don't—"

I put up one finger. "Wait a minute. You also had the same woman when your dick slipped and fell into Chase, didn't you? Why does havin' a woman matter now?"

"Because I say it does, that's why."

My face was all scrunched up. I was confused. "Really? You weren't thinkin' like that when you were blowin' smoke into her pussy and suckin' it, were you?"

I could see the twisted look on Roc's face; the truth must've upset him.

"Let me say this to you with no intentional disrespect," he said. "Who I decide to fuck ain't got a damn thing to do with you. When you get done makin' all that noise, no explanation as to why I don't wish to fuck you will be given. If you don't like what I'm sayin' to you, there are five other beds in this room for you to snooze in. Move the fuck away from me, because I'm goin' back to sleep."

Well damn! I guess his Doberman Pinscher-looking ass told me. I now understood what Chase meant about this motherfucker and his teasing tactics. He never should have touched my butt, invited me to play with his stuff, and then told me he'd be gentle when the time came for us to have sex. Not only was I disturbed by his rejection, but I was also embarrassed that I had put myself out there.

At this point, all I could do was pick up my cracked face from the floor and get out of the bed.

"Excuse me for bein' a thorn in your side." I got comfortable in another bed next to him. "I shouldn't have overstepped my bounty, and you don't have to tell me twice to stay in my lane. You were very pacific about us hooking up, but no need to worry about me no mo'."

"I hope not." He turned and looked in the other direction. "And it's *boundaries*, not bounty. And the Pacific is an ocean."

I bit down on my lip and tightened my fists. I was about to go over there and bust that mofo upside his head. No his ghetto-talking, thug-life ass didn't try to correct me again, did he? I couldn't give him a pass on this one, not tonight.

"Listen up, street meat. You can go jump yo ass in the Pacific and nobody would miss you. Don't pretend that you some kind of college professor up in here who can teach me a thing or two 'cause you can't. Bounty, boundaries, or bow-tie pasta, you ain't got no business tryin' to correct me when you have proven yourself not to show or know love for the written word. I will stay in my place, so you can take that crooked, long dick of yours and shove it up your own ass. In other words, go fuck yourself, Roc. I hope it feels good to you, as I had hoped it would feel to me."

Roc refused to turn around and look at me. "Shut the fuck up and go to sleep. I ain't even tryin' to hear all of that noise you makin' right now. Silly."

"Yo mama silly."

He didn't respond. I was fuming inside and wanted to keep it going, but whatever. I had something for him, and I would definitely deliver it soon.

Minutes later, all I could hear were Roc's snores. It angered me that he was sleeping peacefully. I looked at the clock, seeing that it was only 10:45 PM. That was considered too early for me, so I yanked the covers aside and got out of bed. I went into the living room and used the cell phone to call my girlfriend, Portia.

"Hello," she said, sounding like she was smacking on something.

"What you doin'?" I asked.

"I'm on the phone with Tracy. What's good with you?"

"Nothin'. Just bored out of my mind, that's all. Hell House is down to me and this ol' borin' fool, Roc. He's sleepin' right now. I was callin' to see if you would come by to keep me company. You can bring Tracy too, even though I don't care much for her."

"Are you serious?" Portia shouted. "I thought y'all couldn't invite nobody to come over there?"

"We're not supposed to, but no matter what I do, Roc done already lost this challenge. He just don't know it yet."

"Whatever you say. I would love to come over there. Give me the address again."

Even though Portia had dropped me off at Hell House, I gave her the address again. I told her to bring her swimming suit, in case she wanted to take a dip in the pool.

After I got done talking to her, I called Kenny to see what he was up to. Our last conversation didn't go so well, but since Roc had dissed me, I needed somebody to tell me something good.

"Yo," Kenny said, obviously not recognizing the number. "Who dis'?"

"Jada. What you up to?"

"Sittin' here chillin' with Lavel and Poorboy, smoking some Kush."

"Oooo, bring me some."

"Girl, please. Last thing I recall, you didn't even want to tell me where you was at. You only done called me one time, and you know that shit ain't cool."

"Boo, I'm over here tryin' to handle a li'l somethin' so I can win this paper. I couldn't tell you everything upfront because this was supposed to be private."

"Yeah, whatever, Jada. You know damn well that you hemmed up somewhere with another nigga, so stop playin'."

"I just told you what was up. If you don't believe me, you can come and see for yourself. Bring some of that weed with you, and you can bring Poorboy and Lavel with you too."

There was silence, but a few minutes later, he asked me for the address. I gave it to him and then hurried to change into my swimming suit. I wasn't worried about Roc not one bit, but I did my best to keep quiet so he wouldn't wake up and ruin the fun.

Portia and Tracy arrived first. I looked through the window and saw them walking up the driveway. I hurried to open the door so they wouldn't ring the doorbell and wake up Roc.

"Welcome to my palace," I bragged, as if Hell House was my residence.

Portia's and Tracy's eyes lit up like Christmas trees as they stepped into the foyer checking out the scenery. They were dressed in one-piece swimming suits that were covered by fishnet robes. As big girls, none of us could do the bikini thing, but we still looked good. Well, Portia and I did. Tracy, on the other hand, looked casket-ready. She had on too much makeup, and the ruby-red lipstick was not working for her.

"This place is off the hook," Portia said loudly. Her voice was naturally loud, so I hurried her and Tracy to the backyard.

"Girl, why you ain't tell me you was over here doin' it like this?" Portia asked.

"I tried to tell you, but every time we talk, you always talkin' about yourself."

Portia playfully shoved my shoulder, but she knew I wasn't lying. We sat in the lounging chairs to relax. Portia and Tracy appeared to still be in awe. Tracy and I weren't the best of friends, and the only reason we knew each other was because of our friendship with Portia. It didn't surprise me that she hadn't said much. She always hated on people who had something good going on.

"Tracy, why are you so quiet?" I asked. "Are you all right?"

"I'm good. I'm just surprised by how nice this house is. How did you say you got involved with this Hell House thingy?"

"I didn't say, and I'm not gon' say because only certain, special people were invited to come here."

"Aw." She slightly rolled her eyes and looked away at the crystal-blue water in the swimming pool.

"So, girl," Portia said, "tell me what's been goin' on in here."

I started to give Portia and Tracy the Hell House scoop. Their mouths hung wide open. They couldn't believe what had gone down, and they were eager to meet Roc and Jaylin.

"Go wake that nigga up," Portia shouted. "I want to see his ass. If he that fine, he will be goin' home with me tonight."

Portia needed to quit. If Roc wasn't interested in a fine bitch like me, then he definitely wouldn't go there with a trick like her. I was being nice when I said she looked nice, but truthfully...her lips were black from smoking too much and her blonde weave looked six months old. When this challenge was over, I was going to take my best friend to the beauty shop. Her hair was a hot-ass mess and she needed a complete makeover. She kept on talking about what she would do with Roc, and as she kept talking, my eyes kept shifting to the tracks that were showing in her hair. And was that a booger in her nose I saw? I hoped not. I didn't have the guts to tell her something was hanging from her nose.

The ringing doorbell knocked me out of my thoughts. I quickly jumped up from the table and told Portia and Tracy that I would be right back.

By the time I had reached the door, I could see Kenny banging on it like he was the police. I pulled the door open, but calmed my attitude when he stepped forward to give me a hug.

"What's up, sweetness?" he said, squeezing me tighter.

I couldn't help but to smile, even though Kenny smelled like a gang of liquor mixed with weed. The smell tickled my nose, almost giving it a sting that burned. His friends had the same smell too. I hoped these doggone fools were stable.

"Let me make one thing clear," I warned. "Don't y'all be comin' up in here tryin' to take nothin' or tear nothin' up. There are cameras all around here, and the owner will prozecute."

"Prosecute, girl," Poorboy said with a frown on his face. "I know about that all too well, but just so you know, I don't get off on petty things in people's houses."

"Same here," Lavel added and cuffed his dick. "Just point me in the direction of the party, so I can get on some of these hoes up in here."

"Ain't nobody here but Portia and Tracy. I can assure you that they ain't no hoes."

"Shiiiit," Poorboy said. "If you talkin' about yo friend, Portia, then she is a hoe. She waxed me and one of my boy's dicks several times."

"I doubt that, but you need to take that up with her, not me."

I walked off feeling a bit irritated. Kenny smacked my butt hard, causing me to quickly turn around.

"Damn, baby. Nigga ain't seen you in a while. You gon' give me a kiss or somethin', ain't you?"

I blushed and was unable to downplay how happy I was to see him. We'd had our problems, but he was sweet in his own little way. Besides, my rent needed to be paid by Monday. I was going to ask him to take care of it for me. He wasn't the finest dude I'd ever dated, and I wished that he'd kept his beard trimmed better. It was a bit on the rough side, as was his hair that he always sported in a short Afro. A gold grille was displayed with every smile, but the one thing I did appreciate about Kenny was the way he dressed. He rocked name-brand clothes from head to toe. Most of his clothes were casual—jeans and T-shirts. His jewelry set him off, and tonight he wore a gold chain that hung about seven inches from his neck. I forgot to tell him to bring his swimming trunks, but I was sure that if the fellas wanted to swim, they would do so in their drawers.

It didn't take long for the party to get started. I cranked up the music, and after tossing back a few drinks, Kenny and me started dancing. The others sat around getting high and drinking. I couldn't tell anyone how many trips we'd made to the bar in the game room, but there were plenty.

"Y'all muthafuckas should've told me there was a pool here," Poorboy said, removing his shirt and hanging jean shorts. His fat butt jumped into the pool, causing a huge splash that damn near washed all of us away, as we sat nearby.

"Damn, man" Kenny griped. He jumped up from the chair. "You got my shit all wet."

I couldn't help what I was about to do, but Kenny always looked like he could use a little water. I rushed up from my chair to push him in the water, but slipped and fell on the concrete pavement. No one could contain their laughter, not even me who was beyond fucked up. Kenny strained to lift me in his arms, but with his arms secured around me, Lavel wound up pushing both of us in the water. I couldn't swim, but I knew how to float. I wiggled my way to the top, where I could see everybody cracking up.

"Now, that's how you push somebody in the water." Lavel swiped his hands together. He was so busy paying attention to us, that when Portia pushed him in the water, she caught him off guard. We all laughed. He splashed water on Portia, drenching her as well. She ran away from the splashing water, but I just shook my head when I saw the crack in her flat, wide ass swallow the swimsuit.

"Girl, get yo swimsuit out yo butt," I yelled. "That sucker done crawled way up in there."

"Then stop lookin' at it," Portia yelled back. She pulled the swimsuit out of her butt. "If you wasn't lookin' then you wouldn't have noticed, hooka. I hate a jealous bitch who thinks she's all that."

"Hooka or whatever, you need to go sit down. With your legs rubbing together like that, they may grease up and start a fire. If they do, I'mma have to pull out the chicken wings and start frying them, boo."

"And I'mma have to knock the shit out of you for soundin' so ridiculous. Don't say nothin' else to me, Jada. Trust me when I say you about to get yo feelings hurt."

See, that was why I never told my friends when they went around looking like damn fools. Everybody always had something smart to say. I kept my mouth shut, until I felt Kenny come up from behind me. He put his arm around my waist and pulled my earlobes with his thick lips.

"I want some loving, girl. You lookin' real good in that swimsuit and that fat ass of yours got my dick dancing. You feel it?"

He grinded against me, but truthfully, there wasn't much for me to feel, other than his potbelly stomach. I hated to be so negative, but the truth was Roc had me in a bad mood.

"Yeah, I feel it. I'mma take care of that for you real soon, but back up 'cause I'm a little hot right now."

"Keep it hot, all right? Real hot."

I released a fake laugh and exited the pool. I was glad that my hair was braided to the back, that way I didn't have to worry about it being all over my head. I picked up a towel to dry off and then sat between Tracy and Portia, who didn't want to swim. The fellas were getting it in. They kept busy by playing volleyball in the pool.

"This is the life," Portia said, changing the subject and forgetting about our little squabble. "I could live here forever. You gon' hate leavin' here, ain't you?"

"Yes and no. I kind of—"

I paused to turn my head because I noticed Tracy's and Portia's attention focus elsewhere. I saw Roc coming our way, displaying a frown.

"Oh boy," I whispered underneath my breath. "I hope we ain't been that noisy."

Portia patted her weave like that was supposed to make a difference. "That chocolate muthafucka is fine! I surrender the pussy right now, goddamn it, right now!"

Tracy high-fived Portia as Roc approached the table with no shirt on and muscles in full effect. His pajama pants hung low on his waist and Jordan sandals were on his feet. Too bad his face was twisted from anger, though. The facial expression wasn't a good look for him, but that was just my opinion.

"What the fuck is up with you, these people, and the noise?" he barked.

I pulled back a chair for him to sit. "I know damn well that Jaylin ain't done rubbed off on you, has he? You soundin' more like him instead of yourself. Sorry about interruptin' yo sleep, but you were so borin' that I had to invite some of my peoples over here to keep me company."

Roc's eye twitched as he narrowed them to look at me. I guess he figured I had lost my mind, but that was in no way the case.

"Yo ass is done, Jada. Cooked," he threatened. "You done fucked yourself, so have all the fun you want to tonight, because this is it for you."

"I don't think so, baby, but, uh, go clear your throat. We'll talk more about this tomorrow afternoon. I'm entertainin' my guests right now. If you're not interested in smoking some of this fire weed with me and gettin' blasted, then I suggest you go back inside and cuddle with your pillows. I'll be in there later to read to you again, but don't wait up for me, okay?"

Roc had a look like he wanted to punch me dead in my face. But when Poorboy called his name, he snapped his head to the side. A slight smile covered his face. I was glad about that.

"What's up, nigga?" Roc said and then walked over to the pool.

They sparked up a conversation. I overheard Poorboy mention something about Roc's mechanic shop. I assumed that's how they knew each other. Kenny and Lavel just listened in.

Portia started fanning herself with her hand. "I can't believe that's Roc. You mean to tell me that you've been living here with him and you don't have any juicy stories to tell?"

"Not one about us, but I told you about the other bitch who

was up in here. Roc be actin' too funny. You gotta catch him when he's high. I can't stand men who be up one minute and down the next. He too wishy-washy, and you don't always know what to expect."

"He'd be down all right," Portia said. "Down in this pussy doin' exactly what I want him to do with it."

I didn't bother to comment. Saying the wrong thing would set her off. The only thing she needed to be down with was a rag. One of these heifers was musty. I had a very sensitive nose that didn't appreciate foul smells.

"Rooooc," Portia called out to Roc, trying to get his attention.

He turned his head. "Hold up a minute, ma. I'm comin'."

"I'm cumming too, baby. Hopefully."

Portia was giddy as ever. She could barely contain herself. As long as she didn't raise her arms, I guess she was okay.

"Can you answer somethin' for me?" I said to Portia.

"What, girl?"

"Why do some women be actin' so desperate and thirsty every time they see a good lookin' man with a big dick print in his pants? You would assume that with a big one, he already got a woman, wouldn't you?"

"Not necessarily," Tracy said. "And ain't nothin' wrong with a woman goin' after a man who look good and who packaged up the right way. That's what we want, don't we?"

"Right," Portia said, rolling her eyes at me. "Jada, you always tryin' to talk about somebody, but I bet any amount of money that you done attempted to get at him too."

"Maybe I did attempt to, but it ain't like I'm gon' have a heart attack just from seein' a fine dude. You over there sweatin' and gaulkin' at him like he a piece of sirleon steak or somethin'."

"He look better than sirleon steak to me, and I hope he as juicy as one too."

"What the fuck is sirleon steak?" Tracy said. "I thought it was *sirloin*? And if y'all want to go there with the steak thing, he's more inline with a porterhouse, ain't he? That's way more juicier."

Portia broke Tracy down before I did. "What-the-fuck-ever, Tracy, you know what we meant. Regardless, he juicy lookin', and I wouldn't mind having that meat caught up in my teeth. Now, shut up because he on his way over here."

"What's up?" Roc said, rubbing his waves.

I hated a nigga who knew he was fine, no matter what. Portia shot him a weak line. "Don't I know you from somewhere?"

"I know a lot of people, so there ain't no tellin'."

"Aw, okay. But, uh, my name is Portia, and this here is my girl, Tracy. You already know Jada, and we like best friends."

"Sorry to hear that, but nice to meet you, ma. I'm goin' back inside to get some shut eye. Have a good time tonight, but please keep the noise down for me."

"I'll do my best, but can I come sleep with you? I'm a li'l tired too. Rest may be what I need."

He blushed, knowing damn well that he wanted to throw up. "I doubt that I'll be able to rest with yo fine self in the bed with me. So, I'mma have to pass this time. If we happen to meet again, holla at me."

She was all smiles. Roc hit her with the deuces sign and went back inside.

"I told you I could get that if I wanted to," she screeched. "Now, what you got to say about that?"

"What I got to say is he just broke you down gently and tried not to hurt your feelings. Don't get what he said twisted. I bet you any amount of money that if you go inside and attempt to get in the bed with him, his ass gon' treat you like a bottom-of-the-barrel bitch. He'll fuck with yo head, no doubt, but that's it."

Kenny didn't appreciate all the talk about Roc. Jealousy was locked in his eyes. "What's up with you and that nigga?" he asked. "Is that who you've been here with?"

"The only person I've been here with is myself. Stop bein' so jealous and let's get busy on this card game. Are y'all down or what?"

After the fellas took off their wet clothes and were down to their boxers, we started playing cards. The games we played went on for a few hours. I had drank so much alcohol that I needed to go pee. I rushed into the bathroom, and as soon as I came out, Kenny was waiting for me.

"Fuck that card game," he said. "Let's go somewhere private."

His eyes were almost closed from being drunk as well. They were so narrow that he could barely see. Not only that, but he was just as horny as I was. I threw my arms around his neck. We laughed and kissed our way toward the bedroom. Roc was in there asleep, but maybe he wouldn't mind. The moment I busted through the door, I heard him snoring.

"Shhh," I said after breaking my kiss with Kenny. "Be real quiet and don't be talkin' no freaky mess while we doin' this."

He nodded, but I giggled because I knew he would talk shit. I fell back on the bed, watching as he yanked his boxers down to his ankles and stepped out of them. His dick was at attention, but it sure as hell didn't look as good as Jaylin's or Roc's. I tried to wash away the thoughts of their dicks from my head, and when he smiled, so did I. I pulled the cover over me and removed my swimsuit. Kenny joined me underneath the cover, causing the bed to squeak loudly as he maneuvered in between my legs. He wasted no time slipping his short meat into me. It felt more like a thick finger than it did a dick. And whatever happened to foreplay? This was ridiculous. The only reason I went along with the ride was because I had to break the news to him about paying my rent. If it wasn't for that, this wouldn't even be happening right now.

Kenny picked up the pace, but all that caused me to do was laugh.

"That tickles," I said, giggling. "Plus, you makin' this bed squeak too much. Slow down."

He paid me no mind. He kissed my cheek, and in order to slow him down, I wrapped my legs around his back. That caused his long strokes to become shorter. I could feel more of him, but I closed my eyes to get a vision of the video I'd watched with Roc, Jaylin, and Chase. I wondered why my sexual experience couldn't go down like that. Why couldn't Kenny caress my body like Jaylin had done to Chase's? Why wasn't Kenny kissing me like he kissed her? Hell, I wanted Kenny to massage my body too, just so I could open my mouth and drop my head back in pleasure. But that wasn't happening here. Kenny was heavy and lazy. He was huffing and puffing like he was ready to blow the house down, and hadn't done a damn thing.

The only way this was going to get better was if I pretended that he was Roc or Jaylin. I went with Jaylin, since Roc had pissed me off. Within minutes, I was starting to feel it.

"Yeah, baby, work that dick," I said, starting to grind my hips. "Dig in there like you searchin' for gold."

I slapped Kenny's ass hard, causing him to halt his strokes.

"What the fuck you doin'?" he shouted. "That shit hurt!"

"Sawry. I was so into this, so forgive me. Continue. Please."

This time, I rubbed Jay…I mean, Kenny's ass, instead of smacking it. In my head, his dick grew bigger and bigger, causing my loud moans to escape throughout the room. The bed rocked faster and faster, as I had finally joined in with more movements.

"This pussy is so juicy and wet. I can't remember a time when you were ever this wet, girl. Damn, you feel good."

"You feel good too, Jay...Kenny, as always."

He slowed his strokes and cocked his head back. "Jay?" he questioned. "Did you just say Jay?"

The sound of Kenny's loud voice caused Roc's snores to end. I saw his shadow sitting up in bed, but I was trying to get mine before all of this came to an abrupt end. I rolled on top of Kenny, but covered myself with the sheet. Hopefully, *Jaylin* would appreciate the ride.

"What I said was I feel so good that I want to sing like a jaybird. Now quit talkin' and let me get done with you."

I bounced up and down on Kenny so fast, making him grunt loudly. "Aww, shit!" he said and then slapped my ass. "Get it, Jada! Do that shit, ma, and make a nigga bust this nut!"

I guess Roc had heard enough.

"What the fuck?" he shouted. "I seriously cannot believe this bullshit. Have you lost yo muthafuckin' mind or what?"

I kept riding Kenny, but turned slightly to the side to address Roc's concerns. "Hold that thought. He gon' be done in about one or two more minutes. After that, this gon' be a wrap and you can go back to sleep."

Kenny ol' five-minute self had the nerve to laugh. So did I, but Roc didn't think it was funny. He went into the closet—I assumed to find some clothes. Meanwhile, I got back to *Jaylin* and rocked him into a coma. I felt a tickle, so I reached out for Kenny's hair and pulled on it. He squeezed his eyes and could barely catch his breath.

"Polish that mutha up, bitch! I want all of it, ya hear me! Every drop of it!"

"Here you go, nigga, here it comes! Yesssss!"

My body jerked, juices flowed, and my toes curled. After that, I collapsed on top of Kenny, but I could see Roc walk by from the corner of my eye. The door slammed and Kenny and I busted out laughing. We were spent. Kenny really thought he had done something. He looked to be on cloud nine. I rolled over in bed next to him, but I was so out of it that I wound up crashing to the floor. Kenny playfully jumped on top of me and started tickling me.

"Oooo, stop! Stop," I laughed. "You gon' make me pee on myself. And if I do, I'mma do it right on you."

He stopped tickling me and stood up. He helped me off the floor and we both sat on the bed.

"How much longer you gon' be in this house?" he asked.

"Not much longer. I'll call to let you know for sure, though."

"That's cool. But you know you should've told me that you were comin' here. It was foul for you not to say anything. I straight thought you had jetted somewhere with yo ex."

"That wasn't the case at all. It was all about gettin' some paper. I do believe that I'm goin' to win this challenge. Until then, I need a favor."

Kenny scratched his head. "What's that?"

"I need for you to stop by my rental office tomorrow and drop off my rent payment. Can you handle that for me?"

He shrugged. "I guess, but you need to make sure I get some of my money back. And don't go talkin' that mess about givin' yo pussy back, because as good as that shit was, you can't have it back."

I laughed. Kenny knew me all too well. At least, he was willing to pay my rent, but he should have known from the past that I wasn't going to give him one dime of his money back. Then again, if/when I won this challenge, I would kick him out a little something, just because.

We talked for a while longer and then left the bedroom to join the others. Roc was now on the living room couch, lying down. I couldn't tell if he was asleep or not.

"Roc," I whispered, but he didn't answer. I guess he was mad, but I would deal with his concerns in the morning.

For now, I had to deal with the people I'd invited to come over. The backyard was a mess. The music was thumping louder, empty bottles of alcohol were on the tables, thick smoke filled the air and two lounging chairs were floating in the pool. According to Portia, Lavel tried to prove that he could stay afloat in the chairs. Knowing that I would have to clean up this mess, I wasted no time pointing to the front door.

"All of y'all need to leave. Why in the hell would y'all mess up this place like this, knowin' that ain't none of y'all gon' stay and help me clean up?"

Portia stood and grabbed her purse from the chair. "You're so right about that, so come on, Tracy, let's go. Besides, y'all took too long. We had to do somethin' to keep ourselves busy."

Tracy and Portia made their way to the door. Kenny, Poorboy, and Lavel did too. I expressed my concerns to all of them about drinking and driving.

"I'm the designer driver," Tracy said. "I only had a few drinks, so Portia and me are good."

"Ugh," I said, getting Tracy's dumb self back from earlier. "You ain't no designer driver, you mean *designated* driver, don't you?"

Tracy cut her eyes and smirked. "You know what I meant. I've been drinking too much, that's all."

"Yeah, whatever, but all of y'all need to be careful."

"I'm good," Kenny slurred. "After that you know what, I'm real good. I've been way mo' fucked up than this, so you don't need to worry about me. Just hit me up in about an hour. I can promise you that I'll be home. In the meantime, you need to hurry up and get there too. We need to finish what we started in the bedroom."

As long as I could bring my jaybird with me, we'd definitely finish up. I walked everyone to the door to say goodbye. I gave Kenny a kiss, but turned his keys over to Lavel who looked more stable than he was. After they were all gone, I locked the door. I made my way down the hallway and glanced at the clock on the wall. It was after four in the morning. I was too tired to clean up. On my way to the bedroom, I spotted Roc who was now sitting up on the couch with a mean mug washed across his face. The cold look in his eyes said one thing—I was in deep trouble. Or, at least, that was what he thought. He was the one in trouble, and I was preparing myself to cook his last supper.

Turn a woman down and what does she do? Go crazy, call you names, and act a goddamn fool. Men, on the other hand, we get turned down and have to deal with it. On a for real tip, Jada pissed me off, but I was too tired to deal with her last night. The last thing on my mind was fucking Jada. She was out of control. I wondered why Jeff hadn't busted up in here to shut that shit down. That was kind of odd, but maybe the motherfucker was trying to get some sleep like I was. I was definitely going to make it my business to let him know what was up. Jada had set herself up for a big downfall. It was now just a matter of time before this would be over.

I guess she thought I was a fool. I had heard her on the phone while in the bathroom, talking to Chase. For now, I decided to play right along with her, but this challenge was a wrap. She had broken the rules. Sometime today, I was going to call her out on what she'd done and tell her to vacate the premises on her free will. If not, Jeff was going to be called to do his so-called investigation. After that, I would be able to get back to my woman, my kids, and to my shop that I'm sure was suffering because I wasn't there to run it. I would have some extra cash in my pockets and bragging rights would belong to me.

I got so uncomfortable on the couch that I returned to the bedroom around six in the morning. I went back to sleep, but when I got up, I struggled to get out of bed. Jada was already up. I suspected she was either high from sex last night or she was still tripping about what had gone down with us. Either way, I changed into my workout gear, and while in the bedroom, I looked around to see if I could find the cell phone she had been using. I searched around the bed she'd slept in and looked through her clothes in the closet. I found nothing until I picked up a pair of her tennis shoes and found the phone hidden inside one of them. Bingo. I turned the phone on and kept it with me.

My workout lasted for about an hour. Once I was done, I passed through the kitchen to make my way to the shower. I saw Jada cooking. She didn't say one word to me; I didn't say nothing to her. I got busy in the shower and then changed into a wife beater and hanging B-ball shorts. Before putting the cell phone in my pocket, I checked to see if any text messages had been sent to her. There were none, but there were several outgoing phone calls to the same number, and a few incoming calls from a different number. I figured the number was Chase's. I wasn't sure what she and Jada had to holler about, and it surprised me that they'd been keeping in touch. Regardless, Jada had possession of a phone she wasn't supposed to have. That alone was enough to end this today, in addition to the party she'd had.

I was ready to get my grub on, so I made my way to the kitchen. Jada was already sitting at the kitchen table eating. What was supposed to be my food was still on the stove. The bacon was burnt, the scrambled eggs were soaked in grease and gobs of black pepper were sprinkled on top. In the toaster were two pieces of bread, burnt to a crisp. When I lifted the spoon that was stuck in the grits, I saw that the grits were full of lumps. It was apparent that Jada fucked up breakfast on purpose, but I didn't trip. I piled the food on my plate and sat right next to her at the kitchen table. She should've been done eating her food, but she hadn't eaten much because she wanted me to see how her food looked nothing like mine. Her food was hooked up. She smacked while licking her fingers.

"What happened to my food?" I asked as I scraped the burnt toast with a knife. I spread jelly on top and bit into the toast.

"I don't know what you mean," she said.

"You know what I mean. Look at my food. You ain't never served me nothin' like this."

"And you ain't ever served me period. Just be grateful and shut your mouth."

I sucked in my bottom lip; my blood was definitely boiling. "Who the fuck do you think you keep talkin' to? I put up with yo bullshit last night, but today is a new day. Watch yourself or else."

She dropped her fork on the table and swiped her hands together. "Or else what? What you gon' do? Hit me?"

"I'm sure you would like that; after all, you seem to be used to niggas kickin' yo ass. Take that aggression you got elsewhere or save it for those fools who be bumpin' you upside yo head, like the one who was here with you last night."

I got up from the table and went into the living room to eat. It was messed up that we had gotten to this point. I thought she was good people, but something about her had changed.

Minutes later, she came into the living room and put her plate on the table.

"I'm not tryin' to be mean to you, Roc, but puttin' Kenny aside from all of this, you did play me last night."

I finished chewing the bacon, but left the eggs alone because they were too greasy. "How did I play you? All I said was I didn't want to have sex."

"But you said earlier that you would be gentle with me. I took that as we would hook up. I never would've put myself out there like that had I known you weren't serious."

I wiped my mouth and rubbed my hands together. Maybe I shouldn't have led her to believe that something would go down.

"My bad for sayin' that to you, all right? I thought you were playin'. I didn't know you were serious about gettin' your freak on with me."

"I had been playin' up until last night. But we both know that you ain't attracted to nobody like me. Women like Chase can get it. But down to earth, witty, and thick girls ain't yo cup of tea. Let's be real."

"On a for real tip, that ain't true. You need to build up confidence and stop comparin' yourself to Chase. It sounds like this has more to do with your self-esteem than it does about me."

She shrugged. "Maybe, it does. But you still rejected me. That kind of hurt my feelings. That's why I called Kenny, but that li'l thing between us last night wasn't about nothin'. A bitch like me still horny, so you know somethin' wasn't right with him."

"I couldn't tell by the way you were hollerin' and screamin'."

"I was fakin' it. Don't you know what a woman sounds like when she's fakin' it?"

"No, I really don't, but that's yo business, not mine. And, FYI, I didn't reject you. I just made a decision not to cause no more harm to myself."

"So, you were willin' to do harm and take a risk with Chase."

I nodded, trying to leave it there, but Jada pushed.

"Then how can you take a risk with her, but then decide not to take a risk with other people? I'm just askin', because the way y'all men process things is kind of fucked up."

"I'mma throw that right back at you, 'cause y'all women got issues too. I can't believe how upset y'all get when things don't go y'all way."

She giggled and laughed as she clapped her hands. "We can be somethin' else, but I'm that way because I believe in playin' fair. That's all."

Jada didn't have me convinced. She knew damn well that she wasn't playing fair with the cell phone or with the party she'd had. I don't know why she thought I wasn't going to hold that against her. Thing is, she hadn't even played fair with breakfast. I decided to call her out on it.

"My mouth tastes like I've been eatin' tar. I don't call what you cooked for me as playin' fair, especially when yo breakfast lookin' like it came straight from IHOP."

Jada looked at my plate that still had most of the food on it. She shook her head and busted out laughing. "I did do you wrong, didn't I?"

"No doubt, but I'll find me somethin' else to eat later."

"You don't have to. I'll hook you up in a minute, but in return…" Jada paused and smiled. I knew what her smile was all about.

"In return," I said, clearing my throat, "you would like for us to have sex, right? Even though you got down with Kenny, you still think we should go there."

"I told you Kenny wasn't about nothin', so why not?"

"Sounds like Chase done rubbed off on you. Don't let her get into yo head like that because she's a bad influence. You seem like you got somethin' to prove, but I think you're much better than that."

I could always tell whenever a woman was being real with me

or not. Truthfully, I did not think Jada wanted to go there with me sexually. If anything, she wanted to brag about it to Chase or she wanted to make herself feel accomplished. She didn't come off as the kind of chick who would fuck any man just because. I saw her as a dick-teaser with a whole lot of mouth. Still, she went on and on about why we should get our fuck on, so I went with my gut and decided to put her to the test. I stood right in front of her and removed my shorts. I tossed them on the couch along with my wife beater. A serious look was on my face.

"Come on. Take your clothes off."

Jada's eyes dropped to my package that wasn't hard yet.

"Stop lookin' at it," I said. "It'll get hard as soon as you take off your clothes and open your legs, so I can get a peek at the goodies."

Jada sat speechless. She reached out to touch my six-pack and then she rubbed the smooth hair above my shaft.

"You is hella sexy, but ain't no way I'm gettin' naked in front of you. We gon' have to be in the dark or somethin'. I don't want you to witness all this cellulite I'm representin' on my thighs and ass."

"Cellulite is no problem for me. If you want to cover up, let's go to the bedroom where there are plenty of sheets for you to cover up like you did last night."

I walked off, knowing damn well that Jada wouldn't follow me. If she did, she would come up with another excuse. Surprisingly, she did follow me, but when I lay back on the bed with my hands behind my head, she didn't budge.

"What's the hold up, ma? You scared or what? Come on and hook a nigga up."

Her eyes scanned me while lying on the bed. She stood, biting her nails. "I'm not scared at all. I just don't think you really want to do this."

I sat up on my elbows and looked down at my goods. "*We* really want to do this, so take off your clothes and start ridin' this mutha. I want some of that action you gave ol' boy last night."

She hesitated, so I started to stroke myself. As my dick grew, Jada shielded her eyes and then swung around. "Okay, stop it, would you?" She turned back around to face me and peeked through her fingers. "I really don't want to do this, unless I get to know you on a certain level. Realistically, I don't get down like that with dudes I don't know much about. And even though Kenny didn't satisfy me last night, he still my boo."

"I respect that. From now on, I don't want to hear yo mouth about us havin' sex again, all right?"

She nodded and smiled. I got up from the bed to hug her, but she quickly jumped away from me. "No, siree. Back it up, back the fuck up. I don't want that thing nowhere near me. It's nice to look at, nice to dream about, but that's it!"

I backed away with my hands in the air. Jada's eyes searched me again from head to toe.

"I'm gon' put on some clothes," I said. "But would you please go redo my breakfast? If you don't want to, let me know so I can go make some kind of magic happen for myself."

"I've seen your magic and it ain't pretty. I got you. Just give me thirty minutes or so to hook you up."

I thanked her. She had no idea how much respect I had for her, but unfortunately, that respect wasn't going to stop me from doing what I had to do.

I was known for talking a bunch of mess, but when it came down to sex, I was a big ol' wuss, especially if I didn't really know who I was dealing with. If I did know him, it would be on. I meant every word that I'd said to Roc, even though seeing him naked like that made it so hard for me to walk away. It was best that I did. I could never see myself letting all that he had inside of me. Unfortunately, my little hopes and dreams about what could have been had to remain a fantasy.

I left the bedroom feeling much better. Roc was sweet. There was a part of me that wanted to tell him about what Chase had been up to. Maybe he and I could somehow work this out. Maybe I could get him into the bathroom where nobody would see us and tell him how I thought the remainder of this challenge should play out. The only problem with that was I didn't have a plan. I didn't know if he would be willing to split anything with me or if he would be upset about all the backstabbing that had gone on. Then there was the trust thing. Could I trust him and would he trust me? I struggled with what to do, and I still didn't have any answers when I finished cooking his food.

"Roc," I yelled out. "Yo food is ready."

This time, I made him some waffles, sausages, and eggs. I poured him a tall glass of orange juice and put his food on the table. Couldn't nobody tell me that Jada Mahoney didn't know how to take care of a man. I had messed up with Kiley, but I had promised myself that I would do better.

Roc came into the kitchen without a stitch of clothing on. He glanced at the food and then planted a kiss on my cheek.

"Thanks, ma. When I win this challenge, I'mma do somethin' real sweet for you."

"You can do something sweet for me now and go put on some clothes. I don't understand how you can walk around like that. Baby, you are brave."

"Brave and confident. You should try this too. I promise I won't bite."

"I don't want to spoil your appetite, so stop talkin' crazy and eat your food."

I playfully slapped his back and watched him eat. I kept thinking that there wasn't a chance in hell he would win, unless I changed things up a bit. I thought about it all day, and as we sat outside playing cards, I tried to get a feel for where his head was with all of this.

"I'm ready to go home, ain't you?" I asked.

He observed the cards in his hand and nodded. "You ain't said nothin' that I ain't been thinkin'."

"Then, let's just call a truce and be done with it. Let's call Jeff up in here and tell him that we both win and this mess is over."

He laid a spade on the table, taking my spade. "I don't think he would be down for anything like that and neither would I. You and me like each other, no doubt, but it's every man for themselves."

"I know that, but I don't think it would be a bad idea for us to end this right now. Ain't no tellin' how many more days and nights we'll have to stay here. You don't seem like you're givin' up, and I don't want to either. But we both can walk away with fifty grand in our pockets. What's so wrong with that?"

"That's not how you play the game, ma. It's either you win or you lose. Besides, I'm confident that I can win this thing. I prefer to have a hundred g's in my pocket, instead of fifty."

He was pissing me off. I was trying my best to save this fool, but his ass was being greedy. "I don't get why you're so confident. Do you need the money that doggone bad where you're not willin' to end this and share? I think it's the right thing to do. This is the last time I'mma put my offer on the table."

He looked at his cards and then scratched his head before responding. "I'm not goin' to accept your offer, so don't bother to swing it my way again. This will be over with soon enough. Then you can pack your bags and get back to whatever you were doin' before you came here."

My brows rose. I was shocked to hear him say what he did, but I should've known that a street Negro would be in it for self. All of my thoughts from today went out the window. This wasn't about us coming together to win anymore. It was back to me and that crazy heifer, Chase, who was behind the scenes calling the shots.

My slight attitude was back. I tried not to let it show. I continued to play cards with Roc, and after he won the game, I asked if he would show me some tips in the workout room on how to shed pounds. I had asked Jaylin to help me, but all he did was yell and insult me. I was serious about losing weight. Although I loved my curves, I still wanted to be in better shape. Some people believed that eating the right foods was key. Since I wasn't going to change up anything in the kitchen, I had to seek other options.

"I don't mind helpin' you, but you gotta stick with it," Roc said.

"You can't expect to be in the gym once a month and see results."

"I already know that, Roc. When I get back home, I'm gon' join a gym. I may even get a personal trainer, but for now, I need to start somewhere."

He got up from the table. I followed him to the workout room. Since I was already dressed in a pink T-shirt and black stretch pants, I didn't have to change clothes. It was a little after six o'clock, and I still had a couple more hours before *Scandal* came on. I missed it last week because Jaylin's ol' picky self wanted to watch something else.

Roc told me before we got started that he wanted me to stretch. He showed me how, so I followed by doing everything that he did.

"You don't have to do this for long," he said as we stood side by side on the rubber mats. "Just stretch as many muscles as you can before workin' out."

I stretched my arms in the air and did lunges to stretch my legs. Roc also told me to do a few squats, so I knocked out ten of those. I didn't want to let him know that my calves were already burning, but by the time *Wheel of Fortune* came on, he told me to get on the treadmill next to him.

"Start off slow and walk for at least twenty minutes. And whatever you do…" He had a smirk on his face. "Don't fall off."

"You act like I tried to fall on my ass before. I didn't. That thing was goin' too fast and that's why I fell."

"That's because you made it speed up. Raise your incline settin' to about two or three. Then hit quick start and set your speed at a slow pace."

I did as he told me to. He put his treadmill on the same pace as mine so we could walk side by side together.

"So, what we gon' do after this?" I asked while keeping my eyes on *Wheel of Fortune*. I was trying to figure out the puzzle. So was Roc.

"After this, we gon' do twenty minutes on the elliptical machine and then twenty minutes on the bikes."

"Are we gon' work the weights? Jaylin said not to mix this kind of exercisin' with weight liftin'. He said do cardio one day and weight liftin' on another day."

"That's what a lot of people do, but I think people need to figure out what works for them and stay on that path."

"So, tomorrow, you think we should do the weights or what?"

Roc didn't respond right away. He looked at the TV and shouted out the word puzzle. Unfortunately, his answer was wrong. I cracked up and almost fell again. My laughter, however, halted when he answered my question about us lifting weights tomorrow.

"I can't predict tomorrow. There is a possibility that we may not even be here."

Did he know something that I didn't? Roc was too sure of himself, but he didn't know that his wake-up call was coming.

"I don't want to predict tomorrow either, but I will predict tonight. After I get done with all of this, I'mma take me a hot shower, pour some white wine, and chill on the couch to watch *Scandal*."

"What's *Scandal*?"

I almost fell off the treadmill again when I snapped my head in his direction. This time, I caught my balance by holding the rail. "Are you serious? You mean you don't be checking out *Scandal*? You watched it with me the week before last, didn't you?"

"I probably paid it no attention, but I think I remember somethin' y'all were watchin'."

"Well, it's a TV drama series that got me hooked. On one episode I watched, Kerry Washington, she plays a lawyer named Olivia, she checked the shit out of her boyfriend. She was like…five, nigga get some balls; four, you don't gotta trust me 'cause I damn sho don't trust you; three, I'm cheatin' with the Prez 'cause you can't put it down like he do; two, kiss my ass; and one, get yo crusty-lipped tail out of here. Her lips be twisted, and the way she be workin' her mouth and switchin' be havin' me like *daaaamn, this chick is bad!*"

Roc didn't seem impressed. All he did was shrug. "Sounds interestin', but I don't think they doin' it like that on TV."

"She didn't exactly say it like that, but that's what she meant."

We conversed back and forth, and before I knew it, twenty minutes had gone by. Surprisingly, I wasn't that tired, but my crack sure did feel greasy. My whole body was sweating, but for some reason, more sweat was in the area of my privates. I dabbed my forehead with a fluffy towel and then tossed it on one of the weight benches. Roc waited for me to get on the elliptical machine next to him, so I did. Five minutes in, my legs were burning and sweat spots were all over my clothes, particularly in the crotch area. When I glanced at the mirror in front of us, it looked like I had peed on myself.

"Hang in there," Roc coached as he looked over at me. "Don't slump down and straighten yo back."

I straightened my back and forced myself to continue. Roc cheered me on the whole time, and once the twenty minutes were up, my legs were numb. My arms were sore and my sweaty clothes stuck to my body. I bent over and put my hands on my knees. While taking deep breaths in and out, I eyed Roc. He went over to the bikes. He wasn't breathing hard or nothing. There was barely any sweat on him and he looked ready to go.

"Come on, ma. We're almost done. You're doin' good. Real good."

I straightened my back and stretched it. While holding my waist-line, I dragged my feet across the floor, making my way over to the bikes.

"You said I may not be here tomorrow because you tryin' to kill me, right?" I said.

"Exercisin' will not kill you, so stop complainin' and let's get done with this. Start off slow and then work your way up to level nine or ten on the bike."

I got on the bike; level one was already enough. If Roc thought I was cranking this thing up to level nine or ten, he was crazy. Maybe to level two or three, but that was all he was getting out of me.

"Faster," he shouted while turning his legs so fast that his bike shook. I tried to go fast like him, but after awhile, I started to feel like a heart attack was upon me. My ass was so wet that it was sliding off the seat. My wet palms could barely stay gripped on the handles and sweat was dripping from my forehead onto the floor. I had never been worked this hard in my life. It felt good, though, until my stomach started rumbling and cramping up. Gas was trying to find an escape route. I tightened my butt cheeks and took several deep breaths to calm my stomach. A few minutes later, the cramps went away. I was thankful. I didn't want to embarrass myself anymore than I already had.

"Five," Roc shouted. "Five more minutes, and you, Miss Jada Mahoney, are done. Pat yourself on the back. I may have a few glasses of wine to help you celebrate."

After helping me like this, Roc was now back on my team. I was upset with him earlier, but I liked how he inspired me. Without him around, I never would've been able to pull this off. I watched the timer go from one minute left, to one second. Exhausted, I removed my feet from the pedals and dropped my head back.

"Lord, have mercy," I said, sighing from relief. "I am so glad that this is over."

"Almost." Roc sat on the floor mats in the middle of the room. "Now all you have to do is a few sit-ups. You need to work your stomach area like this."

Roc pulled the wife beater over his head and used it to wipe across the minimal sweat on his forehead. He put the wife beater next to him and then started to do sit ups. While switching his elbows to touch his knees, he kept lifting his feet off the floor. By the time I got off the bike, he was already up to one hundred sit-ups.

"You'll be lucky to get ten of those out of me," I said.

I staggered over to where he was and plopped down on the mat in front of him. I lay on my back and took a few more minutes to rest. Roc was now up to two hundred and fifty sit-ups, so I watched and waited until he was done.

"Your turn," he said, kneeling in front of me to hold down my feet. I knew he was going to push me to do more, so after five sit-ups, I pretended that I couldn't do any more.

"You can give me more that that, Jada. Up and down, ma, up and down."

"Dang, you gotta make it sound so sexual?"

"I don't care how it sounds. Just do it."

I strained to do more, and by the time I got to fifteen, my stomach cramps were back again. I squeezed my stomach, but I could feel a fart wanting to slip out. I tightened my ass and grunted as I forced myself to do another sit up.

"More," Roc shouted. "Come on, Jada, ten more!"

"I can't!" I shouted back.

"Yes, you can. Give me more."

I strained, tightened, and squeezed as I did five more sit-ups.

"Five more!" Roc hollered.

"No. One!"

"Come on, ma. Give it here!"

On my way up to do one more sit-up, I exhaled and several pops of loud air flew out. I looked around and tried to play it off, like I didn't know what had happened. Roc ducked and backed away from me, thinking it was gunfire. At that point, all I could do was cover my mouth.

"Damn, girl," Roc said with a twisted face. "What the fuck was that?"

I removed my hand from my mouth and whispered, "I'm sorry."

He fanned his hand in front of his face. "You really and truly need to go handle that. You got it stankin' in this mutha, for real."

I couldn't argue with him on that. I tried not to go there, but he kept pushing and asking for me to give him more. I stood and pinched my nose, so I didn't have to inhale what I had put into the air.

"Can I go now?" I asked, hoping we were finished.

Roc walked away, looking disgusted. "It's a wrap. We're done."

I walked like a penguin as I made my way to the door. I then hiked up my leg to give him one more silent poot for memories. Afterward, I took his advice and left to go handle my business in the kitchen with some ice cream. My body was hurting so bad; Lord knows I needed a cane to walk.

Roc

I hurried to get out of the workout room and moved into some fresh air that had done my nostrils some good. Jada had gone to shower. I hoped like hell that she got herself together. While I didn't approve of how she got down sometimes, I did like the realness about her. She surely wasn't no phony, with the exception of whatever it was she was doing behind my back.

I'd been thinking about it all day, but before I brought anything to her attention, I needed some privacy. The only place I could get it was in the bathroom, but Jada was in there. The only other place that I suspected didn't have cameras was in the closet. Therefore, I made my way to it and closed the door. I sat on the floor and removed the phone from my pocket. I dialed out to call Desa Rae's home phone. After three rings, my call went to voicemail so I left a message.

"Ay. I wanted to let you know that I'll be home soon. Meanwhile, I had to see what you were up to. I see you ain't home. On a Thursday night, where could you be?"

I ended the call with all kinds of thoughts in my head. Bad thoughts that made me want to get the fuck out of there to go see what was up. Dez being with Reggie was on my mind, and I also thought about Chase doing something conniving too. Hearing Desa Rae's voice would make me feel so much better, but when I tried her cell phone, I got voicemail again.

"Say, ma, where are you? Wanted to holla at you for a second. I'll try to hit you back later."

I held the phone in my hand. When I heard Jada enter the bedroom, I slipped the phone into my pocket. I hurried to grab some clothes and then threw them over my shoulder. When I opened the door, Jada stood in her white silk bra and panties. She was rubbing lotion on her legs. Surprised to see me come out of the closet, she hurried to cover herself with the towel.

"Where did you come from? I didn't know you were in there," she said.

"I was gettin' my clothes together to shower and change. The closet door closed on me."

"Aw," she said still trying to cover up.

Seeing how uncomfortable she was, I went to the door and then turned around. "I don't know why you actin' all shy and everything. From what I can see, you hooked up nicely. A few more workouts like today and you'll be tight."

She blushed and thanked me. I left the bedroom, thinking that she really did have a shapely full figure. Too bad she thought otherwise.

By the time I washed up and changed into some comfortable clothes, Jada was in the kitchen cooking what she called a special, late dinner for the two of us. She pulled back my chair and invited me to have a seat.

"There ain't a Chinese woman out there who can cook chicken fried rice like me. I made some Egg Foo Young patties too, and wait until you taste my gravy. I bet you won't ever go to the Fried Rice Kitchen again."

I sat in the chair and laughed. "If you got Chinese food on lock, my hat will go off to you tonight. Ain't too many people can do Chinese food the right way. When Desa Rae tried to do it, it was jacked up."

She released a deep sigh. "Don't you get tired of talkin' about yo woman? I mean, if you really want to talk about her, then let's do it. My question to you is, how does she feel about your sharp, thick toenails slicin' her ankles underneath the covers at night? You straight up got it going on, Roc, but once I get a glance at those big, crusty feet of yours, it's all over with for me. I would like to know how she handles all those cat scratches you be givin' her."

Jada was tripping. I looked down at my feet and then looked at hers. "My feet are not that bad. They may need some work, but trust me, ma, when I say you have no room to talk."

"Yes, I do. I'm not the one clawin' sheets in the middle of the night and shreddin' them with my sharp toenails. You are. The Chinese lady by my house can hook you up for twenty dollars. If you ain't got it, I'mma buy you a gift card when I leave here."

"Keep it and use it for yourself. With all that crust droppin' from the heels of your feet when you walk, you need to back away from this conversation. Quick."

"I will. Only because your feet are Desa Rae's problem, not mine. The truth is I don't like to be compared to other women. You keep goin' there with this Desa Rae thing, but no matter what, you need to get ready to give me props for my Egg Foo Young. After eatin' this, you will see me as a blessin' in the skies."

Roc cocked his head back. "As a what? You mean a blessin' in disguise, don't you?"

"Uh, no. I meant exactly what I said. Blessings come from the sky, not from a disguise. That sounds real stupid."

"Whatever you say, ma, I'm good."

She walked away, seeming real upbeat. I didn't know what had her so hyped tonight. She fixed my plate and placed it on the table in front of me.

"Don't eat yet. I'mma dim the lights, light some candles, and get us some wine. I'll be right back."

"What's so special about tonight? You goin' all out, ain't you?"

"Excuse me, but this is how I treat men. I love to cater to y'all, especially when y'all are so deservin'."

"What did I do that was so deservin'?"

"My list is so long that I would be here all night tryin' to tell you. Just hursh and enjoy, okay?"

Jada lit the candles, poured the wine, and joined me at the table. She reached out and held my hands with hers.

"Before we eat, close your eyes and let us pray," she said.

I followed suit and closed my eyes.

"Dear Lord, thank you for bringin' us together in Hell House. I've truly enjoyed myself, and I haven't had this much fun since Kiley and me departed. Bless Roc and his family too. I pray that him and Disser Rae have a happy life together. I pray that he likes the food I prepared for him this evenin', and I'm grateful for the cookin' skills you gave me to throw down like this. I ask that you watch over my family, especially my kitten who is at Portia's house with her. I don't know why her house is so nasty, but do what you can to help her work out that situation. Lord, you know I'm not a greedy person, but I ask that you soon send a whole lot of money my way. I want to donate the money and give to some of the people who are way needier than me. I want to pay my bills and buy a—"

I opened my eyes and removed my hands from Jada's. "Amen. You movin' that prayer in another direction, so cut it. It's time to eat."

Jada laughed and slapped my arm. "I know, right. I wasn't gettin' ready to get all up in it."

"Yeah, you were. But you lost me after you went there with the Disser Rae thing. It's Desa Rae."

Jada started to eat and so did I. Unfortunately, the chicken fried rice was not on point. Neither was the Egg Foo Young, and the gravy was too thick. It was so bad that I didn't want to eat it. I didn't want to hurt Jada's feelings, but when she asked if I liked it, I had to be truthful.

"It's all right. I've definitely had better and yo gravy is too lumpy."

"What?" Jada shouted. "Where? Where can you get Chinese food better than that?"

"Several places like The Fried Rice Kitchen. I guess I like the way Chinese people do it. This here ain't doin' nothin' for me."

She dropped her fork and appeared stunned. "You just tryin' to make me mad. I'm not goin' there with you, Roc, 'cause you know doggone well that food is good."

I hated for somebody to tell me how I felt about something, especially when I had my own opinion. "If it's good, you eat it. I'mma opt for a TV dinner and call it a night."

I got up from the table, but before I could pick up my plate, Jada snatched it. She stormed over to the trashcan and dumped my plate.

"I hate picky-ass, ungrateful men. I'm done cookin' for you, and anything else you eat in this house will have to be made with yo own hands."

I didn't bother to argue with Jada. It was all good when I was praising her food, but now I was being ungrateful. She was so upset with me that she didn't even eat. She turned the lights back on, blew out the candles, and went over to the couch with a glass of wine in her hand.

"Are you gon' watch anything on TV tonight? If not, I'm watchin' *Scandal.*"

Just to keep the peace, I joined her on the couch. Thankfully, she was all into watching *Scandal* and her snobby attitude had changed. The only time her eyes shifted in another direction was when a commercial came on.

"It's good, ain't it?" she said.

I shrugged, not really paying attention. I was working a crossword puzzle. "I guess, but I got other things on my mind right now."

"Other things like what?"

Before I could answer, the phone in my pocket rang. I looked at Jada. Her eyes were locked with mine.

"Things like, maybe I should let you answer this, especially since I suspect it's for you," I said.

I removed the cell phone from my pocket, and obviously recognizing it, Jada sat speechless. I glanced at the number that flashed across the screen. It was Desa Rae's number. That wasn't the number I had hoped to see, but I hurried to answer before she hung up. Jada crossed her arms and pursed her lips.

"I see that there's about to be a scandal up in here," she said.

"What's shakin', ma?" I said to Desa Rae while keeping my eyes on Jada.

"Roc? I…I didn't know whose number this was. I saw that you called earlier, but Chassidy and I were at Monica's house. I'm sorry I missed your call."

I wanted to continue my phone conversation with Desa Rae, but I had to make this quick. I didn't want Jeff to see me on camera with the phone on, and I also didn't want Jada to use this against me.

"I hope y'all had a good time, but I can't continue to holla at you on this phone. I'll try to hit you up soon, but just tell me real quick that everything is good with you."

"Everything is fine with me, but I want you to hurry home. I miss you. I don't know how much longer I can go without seeing my Rockster."

I couldn't help but to smile. "Soon. I'll be there soon, all right? For now, I gotta go. Give Chassidy some love for me and mega love to you too."

Desa Rae returned the love, and even though I felt good about our conversation, I didn't feel good about the way Jada was staring at me. I placed the phone on the table and eased back on the couch.

"Sorry for the interruption, but would you care to explain how that phone made it into this house?"

Jada's neck started to roll. "I'm not sure, Roc. Why don't you tell me?"

"Nah, I think you do know, especially since I heard you in the bathroom talkin' to Chase. And I found that phone inside of your tennis shoe. I also saw a friend's number that you've been callin', and why are you callin' Chase so much? Vice versa. And let's not talk about the party you had last night. You know that you broke the rules, right? I'm afraid to tell you that you done fucked yourself, ma. Bad."

She ignored me and looked down at her feet. She then propped them on the table and wiggled her toes. "That lotion didn't seem to help at all. I guess I'll be gettin' the pedicure sooner than I thought."

"I must agree with you on that because you 'bout to have plenty of free time on yo hands."

She snapped her head up and shot me a dirty look. "What is that supposed to mean?"

I leaned forward and placed my elbows on my knees. "It means that your journey ends here. You're done, Jada, because you didn't follow the rules. Either you leave now or leave later when Jeff gets here. It makes me no difference, but either way, you got to get up out of here. Hell House is a wrap."

She squinted to glare at me. "I was startin' to like you, Roc, but if you gon' play me like this, I'm good. I'm not leavin', so you may have to reach out to Jeff and tell him to get over here. Just because I had a phone in my shoe, it doesn't mean that the phone belongs to me. As for the party, I was bored. Now what?"

"I guess the phone belongs to a ghost, then. If that's what you want me to believe, sorry, can't do it. Jeff will determine if the party was a big deal or not. I say it was, but we'll see."

She winced and then barked at me. "Snitch."

Eager to be done with this, I got up from the couch to go shoot Jeff an email. I wasn't sure if he had witnessed what was going on, but my email implied that he needed to get here as soon as possible. I wasn't trying to be no snitch or anything, but this was the only way for me to put closure to this challenge and get my ass home.

After I got done sending Jeff the email, I turned around to look at Jada. She was filing her nails and was tuned in to the TV, still watching the rest of *Scandal*. I didn't know why she wasn't in the bedroom packing. If she thought that Jeff was going to save her ass, she had the rules of this game all fucked up.

Not saying another word to her, I sat back on the couch and waited for Jeff to come. Jada had gotten up to pop some popcorn. Before she returned to the couch, she reached out to hand the popcorn bowl to me.

"You want some," she said. Her tone was sharp. I could tell she was pretending not to be mad, but she was.

"Naw, I'm good. Eat up."

She tucked one of her legs underneath the other and sat down. She ignored me while chomping on the popcorn. Fifteen minutes later, we could hear the front door open. In came Jeff.

Jada kept her eyes on the TV, and as she started laughing, she held up one finger. "Hold up y'all, wait a minute. This episode of

Scandal is so damn good! These people be havin' me crackin' up. I love it when the Prez and Olivia get together. They start playin' that dreadful music in the background. Sexy, but craaazy. And the endings always leave me holdin' my breath."

Jada was tripping. I didn't have time for games. She was doing her best to play them. I stepped up to Jeff, almost blocking the TV so Jada couldn't see. She leaned over on the couch, squinting so she could watch the last few minutes.

"We got a problem," I said to Jeff. "I guess you got my email. There were some people in this house who weren't supposed to be here, and you've seen this cell phone that ain't supposed to be here either. Jada had it. As soon as you make the call, she needs to exit."

Jada rushed up from the couch and stood between me and Jeff. She turned to Jeff, but from the corner of her eye, she was trying to see next week's episode of *Scandal*. Once the preview was over, she gave all of her attention to Jeff.

"First off, Roc don't know what he talkin' about. That phone ain't mine. It belongs to Chase. Pertain' to the people who came to the house last night, I'm sorry about that, but I got bored. I was havin' friend withdrawals."

I hurried to speak up. "Yeah, well, I've been havin' withdrawals too, but deal with it like I have. And Chase's phone or not, you've been usin' it."

Jada swung around to face me. "Obviously, so have you. Weren't you just speakin' to Desa Rae?"

Her eyes rolled and she turned back to Jeff.

"Let's not argue about this," Jeff said, knowing that things were about to get heated. "I know exactly what's been going on. Jada, you have played very unfairly."

Jada winced and held her nose with the tip of her finger. "Jeff, is that your breath smellin' like that? Ugh, you must've gotten a hold to some overly active pus…cooda. Phew." She fanned the space in front of her with her hand.

Jeff was so embarrassed that he backed a few inches away from Jada. His breath was kind of foul, but I wasn't about to call him out on it. I was trying to deal with this shit, but Jada kept trying to prolong her exit.

"I had seafood earlier," Jeff replied in his defense.

Jada didn't buy it. "You had more than seafood, but I'mma save my issues with yo breath for another day. For now, I guess you're feelin' what Roc is tellin' you. You want me to go, right?"

"I'm afraid so. With his vote, you have to leave. I also saw you with the phone too. I think you should go, unless you have a legitimate reason as to why you shouldn't have to."

Jeff stared at Jada without a blink, seeming to give her an opportunity to think of a so-called legitimate reason. She snapped her finger and then turned to me.

"You know what? Stay right there, Roc, I'll be right back. I may have a li'l somethin' to explain my actions, so wait one doggone minute while I go get it."

Jada did the Cha-Cha on her way to the bedroom to get whatever she was talking about. I was beyond frustrated. Jeff looked aggravated too.

"You can expect her to come up with something," he said. "Especially since she's this close to losing and she doesn't want to leave. Before I forget," Jeff extended his hand to me. "Congrats. This wasn't easy, but you hung in there and won. Unfortunately for Jada, she'll have to leave tonight."

Hearing the breaking news made me feel real good inside. I moved away from Jeff and chilled back on the couch. He also took a seat. We waited for Jada to return, which was about five minutes later.

"Okay," she said giddy as ever. She rushed into the kitchen with a large envelope in her hand. After pouring a glass of water, she hurried into the living room with it. She placed the glass of water on the table in front of me and then plopped down on the couch.

"I figured you may need some water after this. And if your throat gets clogged, take some Drano. There's some underneath the sink if you need it."

I sat still as I watched Jada pull out several pieces of paper from the envelope. I didn't realize the papers were actually photos until she placed three of them on the table. To my surprise, two of the photos were of me having sex with Chase. The other one was a picture of me standing in the kitchen with my shorts dropped to my ankles. A wide grin was on my face, while Jada stood in front of me, observing my so-called crooked dick. There was no secret that I had been caught in the act, but what in the fuck happened to people not breaking the rules? No cameras were allowed— period. I hoped that Jeff called Jada out on this.

"Listen," Jada said, having my full attention. "You're speechless and I guess you're thinkin' that we didn't exactly play by the rules." She turned to Jeff whose eyes were glued to the pictures. "Just so you know, me and Chase didn't play by the rules, okay?" He didn't respond, so Jada faced me again. "But here's the deal, Roc. You tripped, fell, and bumped yo head, both of them, too many times. These pictures, and plenty more, will be handed to Desa Rae on a silver platter if you do not pack up yo shit and go. If you do, then I will shred all of this stuff. Desa Rae will never, ever know that her man—no, her fiancé—was up in here slangin' dick. I don't want things to get ugly between us, but realistically, what other options do either of us have?"

I'm not gon' lie, this had me fucked up. I had to take several sips of the water to clear my throat. I put the glass back on the table and licked my dry lips. The pictures were damaging enough, and rules or not, there wasn't much I could do. If we were on my turf, I could have gotten my boys to handle this and wash this mess away in an instant. Jada and Chase would be done with. My mind was running a mile a minute as I tried to think of something to get out of this. I figured Chase was up to some no-good bullshit like this, but Jada being involved caught me off guard. By the time I realized she may have been cooking up something with Chase, it was too late. I tried to play it down like this didn't sting, but no man wanted to be outsmarted by women.

I held out my hands, pretending not to trip. "Aw, Jada, you can do better than this, can't you? You think my woman gon' trip off some pictures that I will deny? Just so you know, she won't, and you can believe that. I'm real disappointed that this is how you've chosen to play your winnin' hand."

"Well, see, my winnin' hand only gets better. And if the pictures ain't enough, maybe Desa Rae will believe me when I show her a video of you and Chase gettin' y'all freak on. No woman in the world wants to see her man tackle another woman's pussy like you did Chase's. And I must say so myself, that you beat that shit up with every bit of your eleven—or is it twelve inches? Chase looked worn out, but not like your mouth did when you blew that smoke… Well, you know what you did. I ain't even gotta say it."

At this point, I couldn't hold back. I rushed up from the couch and jumped on top of Jada. The last time I used my fist to strike a woman was when my son's mother, Vanessa, made me go there. Jada had taken me to that level, but as I tightened my fist, Jeff grabbed it.

"No, Roc, no!" he shouted. "If she presses charges, you'll be arrested!"

I had to think fast. I was still on probation. Something like this could send me back to jail. I was so mad, though, and as Jada laid there with a smirk on her face, it took everything I had to walk away from this bitch.

"Go ahead and do it," she said. "I wish you would put your hands on me."

My chest heaved in and out. I took several deep breaths and then backed away from Jada. The pictures were still on the table, so I snatched them, ripping them to shreds.

"I hope like hell that you recognize what you've gotten yourself into. I will fuckin' kill you over this shit, ma. I mean that on everything that I own."

I threw the torn pictures at her, but all she did was sit up and shake her head. "Nicca, are you on that narcotic or what? I can't believe you're upset with me and you're the one who fucked up. Your shit is messy, Roc. You ain't got nobody to blame but yourself. Your threats don't move me one bit, and trust me when I say you ain't the only Negro with a pistol. Now, getting back to this competition. The last time I checked, the last person in this house is the winner. There can only be one of us, unless Jeff is goin' to make me leave with you."

We both looked at Jeff. He appeared to be in thought. I damn sure didn't want Jada to win. I was counting on him to make her leave too.

"Jada should go," he said without hesitation. "But she can only be voted out of here by you, Roc. I can't make her leave because she broke the rules, only you can. It's up to you. If you say she must go, then she has to go."

This was a bunch of bullshit. Jada knew damn well that I wasn't going to vote her out of here, especially not with her sitting on more of those damaging pictures and possibly a video of me and Chase having sex. Only God knew what else. Jada placed her hand on the side of her face, tapping her fingers against it.

"Tic-tock, tic-tock, the clock is tickin'. Roc, what you gon' do? If it were me, I know what I wouldn't do. I wouldn't risk the love of my life seein' all this stuff, especially not for money. I'd wash my hands, pack up my shit, and be gone. But that's just me. You decide how you want to handle this."

Truthfully, at this point, there wasn't much that I could do but leave. I had to trust that no one would ever confront Desa Rae about this and that leaving here without putting my foot in Jada's ass would be the right thing to do. I also had to accept that this was on me. Yeah, I'd been setup big time, but that's what the hell I get for falling into the pussy trap. I sucked my teeth and released a deep breath.

"I'm out. Done with this, and I expect to never see you or Chase again. Don't come near me or else—"

"Stop with the threats, Roc. As long as you leave, I'm good. I'll keep all that I have in my possessive and no one will ever know what went down in here but us."

"*Possession*," Jeff said, correcting Jada. She went ballistic on him.

"Shut up, please. Let me get him the hell out of here and then we need to talk about my money."

Jeff appeared disgusted. He shook his head, got up, and walked away. I did too, but I stopped by the kitchen to holla at him.

"I need my phone to call a ride," I said. "You wouldn't happen to have mine with you, would you?"

"Unfortunately, I don't. But feel free to use mine. Please don't go far. I need you present for the reunion show."

"I'm not attendin' the reunion show, so count me out. This whole thing got me fucked up. I don't like how none of this shit went down."

"I understand that you're upset, but you agreed to be in attendance for the reunion show, no matter what. I have it in writing that I can sue you if you don't show. You'll owe me ten thousand in damages for not appearing. I don't want to go there with you, Roc, so let me set you up in a hotel for the next day or so. Calm down and come back to do the show. After that, your life gets back to normal and you can put all of this behind you."

I was too pissed to reply. I knew damn well that I didn't want to go home with all of this shit on my mind. Maybe chilling in a hotel room wasn't a bad idea. I definitely had a few things that I wanted to confront that bitch, Chase, with.

With that in mind, I packed my bags and allowed Jeff to hook me up with a cab and hotel accommodations. On my way out, I stopped by the living room to look at Jada who sat with a grin on her face.

"Don't be upset with me, sweetie," she teased. "It was either you or me. I can honestly say that I'm delighted to be sittin' here watchin' you take your walk of shame. I'll see you in a couple of days. By then, I may have my pedicure done that I was tellin' you about. What you think?"

I nodded and sucked my teeth as I glared at Jada. "I think you're full of shit. If you happen to holla at Chase, be sure to tell her that I got somethin' for her."

Jada put her hand close to her mouth. "Oooo, you gon' give her some more? I'm sure she can't wait to get it."

I heard a horn blow, knowing it was my taxi. After throwing up the deuces sign to Jeff, I left out the front door, only to hear Jada screaming "Yahoo" at the top of her lungs.

I hadn't gotten any sleep. All I did was toss and turn throughout the night, thinking about everything that had happened. I was glad that I was at The Marriott, though. I didn't want Desa Rae to see me like this. Knowing her, she would question what was up with me. I was angry and upset with myself for allowing this shit to go down. My hands were tied and I didn't know what to do. It had been a long time since I found myself in a fucked up situation like this. I didn't know how far Jada and Chase would go with the stuff they were sitting on. I was a fool if I believed they wouldn't do anything with it.

As I was in thought, there was a knock at the door. I made my way to it, rocking nothing but my white Calvin Klein briefs. When I looked through the peephole, I saw a Hispanic chick standing next to a cart full of food. I hadn't called room service, so I figured she had the wrong room. Before she knocked again, I opened the door wide.

"I didn't call for room service," I said.

"You didn't, but someone else ordered the food for you. Do you mind if I bring the cart in?"

I figured the food was ordered by Jeff, so I opened the door wider and let the chick come in. She strolled the cart inside, leaving it near the couch in the living room area. When she turned around, her eyes scanned me from head to toe and then traveled back to my package that was on display like a mini mountain. A smile was on her face, and she rubbed her hands together to calm her fidgeting. Finally, her eyes shifted to mine.

"Is there anything else I can get for you?" she asked.

"Naw, but thanks."

I wanted to tip her, but I didn't have any money on me. She made her way to the door, but before she exited, she turned around.

"Lance Gross," she said, snapping her fingers. "Is that who you are?"

I moved my head from side to side. "No. Roc Dawson. The one and only."

Her brows rose and she wet her already shiny lips with her tongue. "Well, good look, Roc Dawson. Are you married?"

"No." I spoke too quickly. "I mean, yes. Well, almost. I am engaged."

The chick smiled at my attempt to get my shit together. I don't know why it was hard for me to flat out say that I wasn't interested.

"Engaged, but not married. That's a good thing, and I may have to stop by later to check on you."

This was my opportunity to clear things up and tell her that stopping by later would do her no good. But all I did was move my way over to the door and open it. I was ready for her to leave so I could get back to my thoughts.

With a grin on her face, the chick walked past me and left. I locked the door and went over to the cart full of food. On top was an array of fruits, pancakes, bacon, and toast. Orange juice was in one pitcher and apple juice was in another. The food didn't look as scrumptious as the food Jada had cooked, but it was doable. I grabbed a piece of toast and returned to the bedroom. While sitting on the bed, I reached for my cell phone and returned a surprising phone call that I had gotten from Chase about three days ago. According to her, we needed to talk. Talking wasn't what I wanted to do, but I dialed the number, regardless, to see where her head was at.

"It took you long enough to call me, but I figured you must've been tied up," she said.

"Maybe so, but what is it that we need to talk about?"

"I'm not sure. I assumed you may have a few questions for me, especially since you now know that Jada and me did some really bad—terrible things to win the challenge. Let me first say that we don't regret anything that we've done. I am sorry that you feel as though we somehow tricked you into all of this, but the truth of the matter is you played yourself."

"Nobody tricked me into anything. And on a for real tip, I don't have any questions for you at all. I suspected that you and Jada were doin' some foul shit, but you know what, ma? It don't matter. Y'all won, so go enjoy the money and have a dope fuckin' life."

I had to pretend that what they'd done hadn't upset me. The objective was for me to remain calm and deal with this when they least expected it.

"The act that you're putting on is not impressive, Roc. I can sense how bitter you are. I know how much it probably hurts you to be put into a position like this, and I'm sure you're worried about your precious Desa Rae. Are the two of you still planning on getting married?"

"Absolutely. Nothin' is goin' to change that, and like I told Jada, y'all gon' have to come better than this. This game is weak, and to be frank, I'm done playin' it. Holla back, Chase. Better yet, lose my number. I don't know how you got it anyway, but move the fuck on and be done with it before you find yourself with dirt coverin' you."

She laughed. "Your threats are hilarious. You would love for me to be done with it, wouldn't you? We'll see, Roc. In due time, we will definitely see if I can move on, or should I say, squash it. Right now, I must tell you that I'm not feeling that option. I still have certain issues that need to be resolved. Whether you accept it or not, you play a huge part in me resolving some of those issues. I'll talk to you soon, but I want you to get all of the rest you need for the reunion show. So, goodbye, and please give my love to Desa Rae."

She hung up. I sucked my teeth, trying my best to calm my anger. I suspected that this bitch was going to do something drastic, so I dialed out to call my boy, Gage.

"What's up, Boss?" he said immediately. "I got one question for you. When in the hell are you comin' home? Everybody been lookin' for you, and Craig runnin' around at the shop like he the Head Negro in Charge. Niggas ain't down with that, so he's been catchin' a lot of heat. You need to get back here to stop the bleedin'. Quick, fast, and I do mean in a hurry."

"When I left, I put Craig in charge, so y'all gotta respect that shit. See what you can do to calm things down for me. I should be there in a few days. Things gon' get back to normal real soon. As for why I hit you up, I need you to do a huge favor for me."

"What's that?"

"I need for you to lay somebody down for me, for good."

"You know that ain't no problem. Just tell me who and it will be done."

"Her name is Chase." I paused because I didn't know her last name. "I need to get more info on this trick. Give me a few minutes and I'll hit you back."

"Cool. Let me know what's up."

I ended my call with Gage, but as I started to reach out to my contact at the police station, someone else knocked at the door. I thought it was the chick from room service again, but when I pulled the door open, I was surprised to see *him* standing on the other side of the door.

"I hope you enjoyed breakfast," he said. "May I come in?"

I wasn't sure what the fuck we had to discuss, but without treating the brotha ill, I opened the door to let him come inside.

Sylvia

When I received a phone call from Jeff, telling me that Jada had won the challenge, I was disappointed. Then again, I was glad that Jaylin hadn't won. Anyone but him was good news, only because he didn't deserve anything but a hard slap across his face.

Jeff advised me that I had to return to Hell House in two days. He also asked me to bring Jada a present for winning. I wasn't sure what to get her ghettofied self, and I had to mentally prepare myself to stand before backstabbing people who all voted me out of the house. I didn't think that seeing everyone again would be easy. But that was minor, especially in comparison to what I was about to do. That was have dinner with my ex, Jonathan. I was surprised that he agreed to it, but there was still so much inside of me that I wanted to say to him. I decided to come clean with him. I wanted him to know exactly how I felt when we last spoke. He'd told me about his engagement, but I couldn't handle the news that day. I was glad that he rushed off to a meeting and didn't notice how torn I was.

But, today was a new day. I was feeling better and I wanted him to know that I was ready to move on. It was now or never.

I sat at Bar Louie in the Central West End, waiting for Jonathan to show. It was almost ten minutes after six. He was late. That irritated me, but no more than when I looked up and saw him strut into the restaurant with a woman by his side. I had gone all out for this occasion. The spaghetti-strapped, purple dress that I wore hugged my curves. My hair was slicked back, but curled on the tips. Several strands dangled along the sides of my face and my gold-hoop earrings matched my bangles and necklace. Plum lipstick moistened my lips, and right before I came here, I stopped at the MAC counter to get the hookup on my makeup and lashes. It was important for me to look at my best, but with Jonathan bringing his woman with him, yet again, I was extremely on edge.

As they headed my way, I couldn't help but to notice how plain she was. She had no curves whatsoever, her long, stringy hair had no bounce, and the only makeup she had on was a loud, red lip gloss that did nothing for her pale skin. Her flimsy dress wasn't hugging a thing and it looked like it came from a clearance rack at the Goodwill. Either way, I smiled and pretended as his decision to bring her was fine with me.

"Sylviaaaa," Jonathan said with a smile on his face. My heart slammed against my chest when I heard him say my name. I swear, I loved this man to death. Truthfully, I had no clue how to overcome my feelings. The deep gray suit he wore accented the minimal gray hairs on his head and the ones mixed in with his trimmed beard. Like always, he was clean cut, classy and sharp as ever. His business attire was always on point and his cologne infused the entire space around us. No matter where he was, he always presented himself as a professional.

I stood to greet him. "Hello, Jonathan. I'm very glad you could make it."

"Me too. My fiancée was on her way out with some friends, so I asked her to stop by to meet you. Lesa, this is Sylvia."

She extended her hand to mine. "Nice to meet you, Sylvia. I've heard so much about you. This is such a pleasure."

Only Lord knows what Jonathan had told her about me, but it didn't really matter. "Same here, Lesa. I haven't heard much about you, but I suspect that it's all good, especially if you're going to be Jonathan's wife."

"I am," she hurried to say. "And I'm looking forward to being the new Mrs. Taylor."

I cringed, hoping that she didn't notice a change in my demeanor. Lesa turned to Jonathan. She gave him a peck on the lips and then told him she would see him later tonight. If I could prevent that from happening, I surely would. After all, I didn't get all dressed up like this for nothing.

"Well, well, well," Jonathan said as he pulled back the chair to take a seat. A smile was locked on his face. I could tell he was as happy to see me as I was to see him. "I must say, Sylvia, that you look spectacular."

"Thank you. So do you, but I would never expect anything less."

He searched into my eyes and rubbed his hands together. It appeared that he had something on his mind, but whatever it was, he switched his attention to the menu on the table. "Let's see," he said. "What shall I order?"

"If my memory serves me correctly, I'll say you'll be ordering the stuffed chicken with broccoli and a garden salad with an extra piece of bread. You'll wash it all down with white wine, and for dessert, you'll consider the chocolate cake. But what you can really have is not on the menu. Personally, I think what is not on the menu may be much more fulfilling."

He laid the menu down and swallowed. I guess he was surprised by my bluntness, but he shouldn't have been.

"That sounds exactly like what I would order, but in reference to what's not on the menu, I'm not interested in that anymore, especially since I recently heard some things about you that concern me."

My brows shot up. "What exactly have you heard about me that concerns you? If your ex wife, Dana, has shared some things with you about me, that shouldn't concern you because you already know how she feels about me. I don't know who else could've said anything to you about me, because we do not share the same friends."

He tapped his fingertips on the table and stared at me. "Interesting. I believe that if you think real hard, you may come up with a name. I'm not going to tell you his name, and you're right. He's my friend, not yours. And just so you know, I was highly disappointed to hear about your actions."

Okay. Now I knew where he was going with this. Jonathan had to be talking about Jaylin. I couldn't believe he had already been in contact with Jonathan to tell him what had transpired between us. I bet he couldn't wait to call and make me look bad, and I bet he didn't tell Jonathan how aggressive he'd been with me.

"Jaylin Rogers, right?" I said. "I'm not surprised that he contacted you, but why does anything he said about me concern you?"

I could sense Jonathan's anger building, from looking at his eye twitch. "It does concern me. I didn't think you were the kind of woman to put yourself out there like that and open your legs up to anyone. Particularly, a good friend of mine who has had numerous sexual partners. Not that it matters, but he didn't call me. I reached out to him about a case I was working on. Your name happened to come up. I was shocked by what he'd told me, and was it necessary for you to go down on him?"

I almost choked on the water I was drinking, but I didn't. If anything, I wanted to get up and run. I couldn't believe Jaylin gave

Jonathan specific details. This is not where I wanted our conversation to go. "To be honest, Jonathan, I don't care what Jaylin told you. I didn't come here to talk about him. I'm here to talk about us."

He was blunt. "There is no us anymore, and even though you didn't come here to talk about Jaylin, I can't help but to wonder how many items you served him from your menu. I'm not happy about you having sex with him, Sylvia, and quite frankly, I think you did it out of spite."

How dare he question me about this, especially when he was the one who had hurt me in the past. Not to mention that he was getting married. I crossed my legs and let him have it too. "No, Jonathan, I did it because I needed a good lay. I suspected that Jaylin would deliver, and bravo, he did. Now, I'll repeat myself again. I'm not here to talk about Jaylin. And while there is no more us anymore, you seem jealous. Is that why you brought your fiancée here tonight? To make me jealous?"

"I brought her here because I wanted you to meet her. I'm not jealous about what happened between you and Jaylin. Again, I'm just disappointed, as well as disgusted."

"So disappointed and disgusted that you prefer we sit here all night to discuss it. If that's the case, maybe we should go. I'm sure you have other things to do with your time, and I must say that I do too."

He was never the kind of man to keep up a bunch of nonsense, so I wasn't caught off-guard when he stood and dropped twenty dollars on the table. "You're right. I do have better things to do with my time tonight. I don't know why I came here, after knowing what you did with my friend. That was low, Sylvia. I never would have done anything like that to you, but I forgot about the kind of woman you really are."

He walked away. I followed, only because I didn't appreciate his attitude about this thing with Jaylin. His words stung a bit too.

"It puzzles me that you still care about who I spend my time with," I said while trailing behind him. He walked so fast that I could barely keep up. I was almost out of breath. "Our relationship has been over with for a while. I'm not the one getting married. You are, right?"

He swung around to face me. "Yeah, I am. And thank God the woman that I'm marrying is nothing like you."

I almost tripped as I rushed out of the restaurant and tried to catch him. He was straight up tripping. How dare he try to throw his hideous-looking fiancée in my face and continue to diss me?

"By looking at your woman, I can tell she's nothing like me. What a shame that is, because I know what kind of woman excites you. I know what a woman must bring to the table to keep you happy. You have no one to blame if you're settling for someone who has nothing in common with me."

He stopped next to his black BMW and placed his hand on the door handle. He remained calm as ever. "I don't do this anymore, Sylvia. Enough is enough. There's no need for us to have these kinds of confrontations, so do me a favor. Don't reach out to me again, okay? You have my word that I'm going to leave this conversation right here. I've said my piece and you've said yours."

"Great. I have no problem not reaching out to you again, so good-bye and good luck."

Taking the high road, Jonathan got in his car and sped off. My car was nearby, so I walked to it with disgust written all over my face. I visualized us having a decent dinner, laughing and talking about old times and then sealing our date with a kiss. Boy, was I wrong. It was odd to me that Jonathan and Jaylin had all of a sudden spoken to each other. I bet any amount of money that Jaylin had reached out to him. This was another thing that I added to my list of reasons why I despised Jaylin so much. He was the devil in disguise.

My high-rise apartment was only a few blocks away. I parked my car in the parking garage, and since my feet were killing me, I removed my high heels and carried them in my hand. With a frown on my face, I waited for the elevator to open. When it did, I got inside. My head hung low, but the moment I lifted it, I saw a man's hand grab the elevator door, as it began to close. Within a second, Jonathan appeared. A blank expression covered his face and he stepped forward. The elevator closed behind him and started to go up.

"I was wrong," he said in a whisper. "So were you, Sylvia. Regardless, I didn't meet with you tonight to argue. I wanted to meet with you so I could look you in the eyes and do this."

He inched forward and reached out to hold my face. His thumbs rubbed my cheeks, as our eyes locked together. Mine were filled with tears. The moment his lips touched mine, a slow tear rolled down my face. I sucked in a deep breath, causing my breasts to rise against his chest. There were no words to describe how I felt as our tongues danced together. There were no words to utter as I felt my pussy throbbing. I couldn't say one word as his hands roamed my body and squeezed me in all the right places. But the one thing that I could say was Jonathan's marriage would never happen if things were left up to me. This night belonged to us, and I was ready to make every single moment count.

Prince

The day that I'd gotten a call from Jeff about Jada winning Hell House, I was in the middle of something and had to call him back. I slammed the phone down to see what the fuck was going on.

"Everybody, on the floor. Now!" the man shouted as I peeked at him through the door in my tiny, corner office. This made the third time within two weeks that some fool done came up in my laundromat robbing my customers. Business had already been suffering because of it. It pissed me off that every time somebody black in the hood tried to run a business, the niggas around here would do their best to shut it down with bullshit like this.

"I want all you bitches to slowly stand up and put your purses over here on the table. Anybody caught trippin' will be dealt with."

Mostly all of the women got off the floor and placed their purses on the table. One lady, however, was tending to her baby and to her son who were both crying. The robber appeared irritated. He scratched his head and rubbed across his crusty lips. Crack-head fool was written all over him, and as I plotted my next move, I was sure I could take him down.

"Shut that goddamn baby up!" he shouted. "And hurry the fuck up with yo purse!"

"I'm sorry, but I can't quiet a baby who's hungry. And my son is afraid. Don't you see that he's afraid of you?"

"Either you shut them up or I'll settle this problem myself! You got one minute to do it or you gon' be lyin' yo fat ass in a pool of their blood."

The crazy nigga rushed over to the table. He picked up the women's purses and dropped them into a huge garbage bag that he carried. Obviously, he came prepared, or at least he thought he did.

I removed the Glock 9 from behind me and held it in my hand. My sidekick, Poetry, touched my shoulder and pulled on it.

"Be careful, Prince" she whispered. "You see that he got a gun too, so be real careful, baby."

"I will, but I need you to stay back. I know how you are, Poetry, but I want you to stay right here so you don't get hurt."

She nodded.

As I made my way out of my office, ol' boy had his back to me. I was able to tiptoe my way close to him. What made him turn around was another little boy in the laundromat who was lying on the floor with his sister. He shouted to the man, "You'd better watch your back!"

With everyone's eyes shifting in my direction, the man turned around. He aimed his gun at me; my gun was aimed at him. While my face displayed a cold stare, he was all smiles, showing his stained, broken teeth.

"Back the fuck up, li'l nigga," he said. "I didn't come here to hurt nobody, but I will if I have to."

"I don't want to hurt you either, but you picked the wrong place to do this shit. I'mma need for you to lay those purses on the table and get the fuck out of here, man."

"Shoot that muthafucka, Prince!" one of my neighbors shouted. "We got yo back!"

The man snapped his head to the side to see who had spoken.

That was when I rushed up to him. He was so frail and weak that it was easy for me to wrestle the gun from his hand.

"Move back," he said, trying to shove me away. "What you gon' do now? Kill me?"

I tucked his gun behind me and kept my gun aimed at his head. "I should blow yo brains out, but consider this yo lucky day. Then again, not so much. Ruthie, Paige and Carmen, handle this nigga. Make sure that he never comes back in here again."

The chicks from my hood, who were also my regular customers, rushed up from the floor and charged at the man fists first. As they waled on his ass, he crouched down and eventually fell to one knee. By the time the other ladies got off the floor to beat his ass, he was flat on the floor. They wore him out, hitting him with everything from their fists to shoes to containers of detergent.

"You dumb-ass fool!" one lady shouted as she stomped the man with her heel.

"How you gon' come in here and try to take our shit?" another woman yelled as she poured bleach on the man.

All I did was watch. Poetry had gotten in on the action too. She used one of my black leather belts to spank that ass like the man had stolen something from her.

"If y'all niggas think this is where y'all need to come to rob somebody, rethink that plan! Be sure to tell yo friends what will happen, if y'all make this move again! You gon' tell them for me, right?" Poetry said.

Ol' boy didn't respond. He was in a cradled position, whimpering like a baby. The ladies weren't backing off of him, and about three to five minutes later, that was when I intervened again.

"All right, y'all, I think he got the message. Let him get up so he can make a move out of here."

Many of the chicks backed away, but the one with the crying baby kept smacking her house shoe against the back of the dope fiend's head.

"One more for my baby and another for my son!"

Whack! Whack!

Finally, she backed away. The frightful man shamefully blinked as he looked around at everyone. "I...I said I was sorry. Damn!"

"Too late for sorry," I said. "Get up and get out."

With blood gushing from his mouth, torn clothes, and one shoe on, one off, the man peeled himself off the floor. He could barely stand and wobbled as he tried to. He limped his way to the door, gripping his wounded side. I couldn't help but to run up to him and give him a swift kick in the ass. He fell to the concrete pavement and I closed the door without feeling an ounce of sympathy. The chicks in the laundromat clapped their hands.

"Thanks, Prince," one lady said. "You know you all right with me."

"Nah, don't go praisin' me. I know now that I betta not fuck with any of y'all in here again. I'm afraid y'all may give me an ass kickin' like that. So carry on, ladies, please carry on. I'm just sorry for the inconvenience, and I hope y'all continue to wash y'all clothes here."

Many of the chicks said they would, but there were a few who didn't partake in the *events* who left. It was all good, though. I had a business to run, with or without them.

I returned to my office that was junky as ever. Some of my washed clothes that needed to be folded were on my desk and I had a pile of quarters that needed to be counted. As I sat in my chair to return Jeff's phone call, Poetry sat on my lap.

"Do you gotta go back to that stupid Hell House thing again? If you do, I want to go with you. I want to see who this bitch Jada is, so I can slap the mess out of her for putting her hands on you."

"I wish you could go back with me, but you can't. Trust me when I say I can handle Jada."

Jeff answered the phone. I asked him what was up.

"The reunion show is in two days. I want to make sure you're here by six o'clock, no later than six-thirty. Since Jada is the winner, I've asked everyone to bring her a gift. It can be whatever you want it to be. Considering what happened between the two of you, you may want to consider the gift as some kind of peace offering."

"Man, fuck Jada. I'll be there by six, and all you gon' get from me is my presence. See you when I see you, and thanks for callin'."

I hung up and leaned back in my chair.

"What you thinking about?" Poetry asked.

"Thinking about what kind of gift I can give to a real special friend who is so deservin'."

"You must be talking about me." Poetry straddled herself on my lap. "I'm deserving of a big ol' kiss and hug, especially after what I did to that man, ain't I?"

I stood and sat Poetry on my desk. "Ma, you deserve way more than a big kiss and hug. And when we get home, I'mma show you all the appreciation in the world. Right now, though, I gotta go take a dump. My stomach is turnin' like a mutha."

She laughed and rolled her eyes as I rushed out of my office. While in the bathroom, sucking in heat from a joint, all I could do was sit in deep thought about my return to Hell House. In a way, I was hyped and was kind of looking forward to it.

Chase

Believe it or not, my life didn't always revolve around men like Roc, who cheated first and then cried about it later. It wasn't about men like Jaylin either, who I used to satisfy my sexual needs. Today was all about me and my girl, Veronica, who I'd gone shopping with. While my money was tight, I could always squeeze a little something out for shopping.

We browsed the shops at The St. Louis Galleria. I wanted to see what I would purchase with the money Jada and I had won, and I also wanted to see what kind of present I could find for Jada. I had to admit that she came through for us. I was worried about her, but at the end of the day, she did what was necessary to get Roc and Jaylin out of the house. For that, she deserved a decent present. I wasn't sure what it would be yet, but a few ideas were floating around in my head.

"Look at these shoes right here," Veronica said as we stood in Baker's. "These are so me, aren't they?"

"They are you and me too, but look at how high the heel is. I'm not sure if I can walk in a heel that high, and the more I look at the shoe, the pink is too loud."

"That's your opinion."

She took the shoe from my hand and asked the sales associate if she could bring her the shoes in a size seven. We continued to browse some more, and when my cell phone rang, I looked at the unknown number flashing across my screen.

"This is Chase," I said.

"Chase who?" the woman questioned.

"Chase none of your business, especially if you don't know who you're calling."

"Why does my boyfriend have your number locked in his phone?"

"No, the question is why are you going through his phone? You sound like another insecure woman. I don't have time for this, and whoever your boyfriend is, tell him to delete my number."

"His name is Rickey. Just so you know, we've been together for ten years, and I have two of his children. So, whoever you are, you are wasting your time, because Rickey Jackson the third is taken."

This was the kind of mess I hated to deal with. I was out with my girl, minding my own business. Now this. I had to step outside of the store to address this foolishness. Some women didn't get it. Whoever this idiot was, she had made the mistake of calling the wrong woman. I had met Rickey almost eight months ago, while Veronica and I were at a casino. We talked, exchanged phone numbers, and he took me out to dinner one time. Even though he was very attractive, I didn't click with him. He didn't have a job, he talked about his mother doing so much for him, and I predicted that he still lived at home with her. Good looks and a big dick print didn't seal the deal for me. I needed way more than that. With that in mind, our conversation went no further. I wasn't sure why he still had my number locked in his phone, but whatever the reason was, his woman was out of line.

"If you want to talk about someone who is wasting their time," I said, "let's talk about you wasting your time with a man for ten years and two children, yet all you can call yourself is his baby's mama. I mean, here you are ten years later, going through his phone and worrying about who Rickey has been talking to or sleeping with. My question to you is how low is your self-esteem? Don't you have something else better to do with your time, and shouldn't you be spending this time motivating the man you've been with for ten years? Get off this phone with me and help that brotha find a job. Do what it takes to get him out of his mother's house. Girl, this is ridiculous, and is the dick that good where you have to resort to calling another woman to see where you stand? Truthfully, I don't recall his dick ever being that good, and just so you know, sex with Rickey was horrible. That's my opinion, and I don't get why you're making a big ol' fuss over a man with a small penis."

By the way she was heavily breathing, I could sense her anger over the phone. "First of all, I'm not wasting my time. And if sex with Rickey is that horrible, then leave him alone. You're the one with low self-esteem. That's clearly the case, because you are out here messing with somebody else's man."

"You mean a man who won't even marry you, right? How many times have you had that conversation with him? Isn't it time for you to put on that white dress and stroll down the aisle to stand hand-in-hand and face-to-face with Rickey? I know you hear that 'Here Comes the Bride' theme playing in your head every day. It's a shame that you'll be four or five babies deep, before the marriage thing may happen. Then, there's a possibility that it may not happen at all. My suggestion to you is to put his phone away and stop calling all of the women's numbers you find. We're not you're problem, sweetheart, Rickey is. The more time you spend focusing on women like me, that's time wasted on you creating an escape plan to get the hell out of that horrific relationship. By all means, it's time to let go."

"Whatever, bitch. Talk all the mess you want to. All I'm going to say is if I ever see you with Rickey, I'm going to kill him, cut his dick off, and shove it down your throat for messing around with him. I may slice you up too, so don't say that I didn't let you know how this is going to go down ahead of time."

"Thanks. How sweet of you to let me know. If that day ever comes, remind me to pat you on the back as they haul your dumb ass off to jail. Those kids you mentioned will be motherless and you'll be the one sitting in jail, wondering why dick meant more to you than your own kids. Now, I have to get back to shopping. If you feel as though you need more counseling, I charge fifty dollars an hour for my services. Check your schedule. If you need more advice, and you got your money in order, feel free to call me again."

I hung up on that crazy trick. I despised women like her who felt brave or bold enough to call another woman with that *leave my man alone* crap. No, leave me alone, because when all is said and done, the man they called about wasn't worth two cents.

I went back inside of Baker's looking and feeling lively. Veronica was sitting down, trying on the shoes she liked.

"Who was that?" she asked.

"A nutcase who ain't worth talking about. So, on another note, what do you think of the shoes?"

"I like them. What do you think?"

She stood and strutted across the floor. I sat there thinking about when she was also in a crappy relationship that we were forced to handle. I'd helped her a lot and we'd been good friends ever since.

"Actually, I like them. Now, all we have to do is find you an outfit to go with them."

"Yep, so turn that phone off and let's get busy. After I find what I'm looking for, we can get something to eat at The Cheesecake Factory."

"Sounds like a winning plan to me."

For the next few hours, we shopped for her an outfit to match her shoes. She hooked herself up and I bought a few outfits too. By the time we made it to The Cheesecake Factory, we were exhausted.

"Remind me to never shop with you again, especially in these high-heel shoes," I said, rubbing my aching feet underneath the table. "My feet are killing me."

"The rule is to always wear tennis shoes when shopping. I don't know why all you cute girls be walking around the mall, shopping with heels and tight jeans on. Your jeans on so tight that they look melted on your skin. Can you breathe?"

"Not really, but you already know that whenever I step out of the house, I always have to look good. I can't leave the house with any ol' thing on. I want to look good in case I meet someone special."

Right then, I looked over Veronica's shoulder at an attractive man who was sitting at a table with another woman. He kept looking at me and then shifting his eyes back to her.

"Well, you know I met Andre while I was at the grocery store with a scarf tied around my head and with a dingy sweat suit on. Thank God he didn't trip. Now, I'm lucky to have one of the best men ever."

I didn't want to tell Veronica that Andre had hit on me before. That conversation had to take place on another day, because I already had too much going on. I kept my mouth shut and allowed her the satisfaction of thinking she had the best man.

"I have to give it to you," I said. "You did luck up on a decent man with Andre. Maybe one day I'll be that lucky too. For now, it is what it is and my search continues."

The man who kept looking at me winked as soon as the woman he was with lowered her head to look at the menu. I smiled and reached into my purse for a pen and dollar bill. I wrote my number on the bill and told Veronica I would be right back.

"Girl, what are you doing? You're always up to something, Chase. You need to quit."

"I know, but I can't help myself. Attractive men with expensive taste excite me."

I laughed and swished my hips from side to side, as I made my way up to the table where the man sat. While standing next to the table, I squatted as if I had picked up the dollar from the floor.

"I think you may have dropped this," I said to the man. "It was on the floor by your foot."

He took the dollar from my hand. "Thanks. I appreciate that, and I'm going to make sure I don't lose this dollar again."

"You're welcome. Consider it your lucky dollar." I got a closer look at the woman, just to check out the competition. I was good—she looked like crap, so I smiled at her. "Enjoy your dinner. The crab cakes are really good. You should try them for your appetizer."

The woman smiled and nodded. "Thanks. Maybe I will."

I walked away with a vision of what the future might hold for me. Some things were positive, but pertaining to my return to Hell House, possibly some negativity too. Regardless, Jaylin would be there. Lord knows I was eager to be in his presence again.

While chilling by the poolside, watching my kids swim, I received a call from Jeff. He informed me that Jada had won the Hell House challenge. My goal was to relax all day, but the news about Jada winning had my mind racing.

"If you would like to, please bring her a present, congratulating her on her win," Jeff said. "If you choose not to bring anything, that's fine too."

"Is there anything else I need to bring, other than myself?"

"No, Jaylin, I'll see you in a few days."

I hung up on Jeff and had to laugh at his comment about bringing a present. I wondered how that news went over with the others. I also thought about what Prince's gift would be—probably a pistol to knock her off. I figured I'd better get all the rest I needed before returning to Hell House, so I laid back on the lounging chair and chilled. Dark sunglasses shielded my eyes, the sun continued to caramelize my body, and the soothing, peaceful sound of the ocean was what I had missed liked crazy. I missed my kids too, but with all of the bickering amongst them, I tried to tune them out.

"Daddy, LJ won't give me the ball," Jaylene whined. "Tell him to give it to me. Pleeease."

I sighed and sat up. LJ had a tendency to pick on Jaylene all the time. I didn't understand why he always liked to hear her whine and fuss.

"LJ, give her the ball back, and take Justin to the other side of the pool. The side you're in is too deep. If you're going to carry him in the water, don't take him on the deep end."

Thankfully, LJ did as he was told. He gave the ball to Jaylene, who ignored it. She started riding in a plastic tow boat with Mackenzie and the two of them splashed water on each other.

Things seemed to settle down, so I lay back again and gulped down some of the iced tea Nanny B had made for us. She was inside cooking dinner. The smell of perfectly seasoned chicken was floating through the air. I couldn't wait to eat, but first I had to deal with Scorpio's slight attitude as she came into the backyard dressed in a skin-tight, red pantsuit that displayed her camel toe. The pantsuit traced her sexy curves, and her long, black hair rested on one shoulder. All I needed to do was find a stripper pole for her to swing on it. I hated to see her dressed this way, but these days, it was all about her wanting attention that she wasn't getting from me.

"I called four times to find out what time you wanted me to pick up Justin and Mackenzie. Just answer the doggone phone, Jaylin, would you?"

Jaylene saved me from going off on Scorpio. Her tone had been outright nasty toward me, but I knew why. It had been a very long time since I'd made love to her. Therefore, she had an attitude about my package being absent in her life.

Jaylene sat on my lap and hugged my neck. "Daddy, I think I got something in my eye. Will you look in there and see what's in there?"

I looked in her pretty eyes that were identical to mine and saw nothing. "I don't see anything, baby. Go inside and tell Nanny B to look in there. Blow your nose too, and wipe your wet feet before you go into the house."

She ran off to go inside. By then, Justin was in Scorpio's arms. Mackenzie and LJ spoke, but they stayed in the pool.

I lifted my cell phone, pretending to check it for calls. I noticed that she had called four times. I didn't approve of her partying and staying out all night, so I ignored her calls. The plan was for me to keep my mouth shut about how I felt. I stopped griping about how Scorpio and Nokea chose to live their lives and stepped back to allow them to do whatever. For quite some time now, my kids, Nanny B, and business were the priority.

"I didn't see that you called," I said, lying. "So please apologize for accusing me of ignoring your phone calls."

She snatched my phone and hit the recent-call button to check the numbers. To no surprise, all of her calls were there. "You are such a liar. Stop playing with me, Jaylin. What time would you like for me to pick up the kids? I'm only concerned because I thought you had somewhere to be."

"I do, but they'll be fine here with Nanny B. So go on and shake that ass in the streets tonight. Yo ass probably won't be able to move with that skintight outfit you got on, and just so you know, I'm not impressed."

"Yes you are. If you weren't impressed, you wouldn't have mentioned it. Just in case you forgot, it was skintight outfits like this that lured you into my bedroom. All that ass shaking got us right here, with two kids, so don't go knocking my sexy appearance now."

I shrugged and held out my hands. "Grateful for the kids, but unfortunately, I didn't know any better at the time. And while you're in the midst of luring all those men to your bedroom, just make sure my kids ain't there. I'm sure they've witnessed yo ass hiked in the air too many times already."

Scorpio opened her mouth wide. She put Justin's wiggly self down and he ran back over to the pool. "Excuse me, but I've only had sex with one man and one man only. My kids don't know who that man is, nor have they ever seen me with him. I don't know where you're getting your information from, but for the record, you are very incorrect."

"One man, huh? I don't know why you're holding back on giving up the goodies. I hope you ain't saving yourself for me. I don't want no more parts of the pussy, and I can honestly say that I've had more than my share of it."

Scorpio rolled her eyes in a playful manner. "Whatever, Jaylin. If I took off my clothes right now, you'd be on it. The only reason you haven't been on it is because you done had so much pussy that your dick refuses to get hard anymore. You done wore that poor thing out. That's the only reason you're rejecting my goodies."

I couldn't help but to laugh. "Ha! Is that what you think? Damn, baby, that's uh, good. Keep telling yourself that. You won't convince me to throw your legs over my shoulders and pound all of this hard meat into you. That's what you want me to do."

Scorpio bent over and moved her face close to mine. "Jaylin Rogers, I don't want you to do anything but continue to take care of your children and pay the bills. You can keep that thing you got slanging between your legs. Fuck up another woman's head with it and see if you can make progress with her. Unfortunately for you, your progress with me has stalled."

I pecked Scorpio's lips and reached out to feel the print of her camel toe. She grabbed my hand and jumped back.

"What's the matter?" I said. "You're afraid that pussy gon' break down and get wet? Go on and have your fun tonight. Don't be partying and thinking about me, and learn to control yourself when you come over here. Your eyes say 'Jaylin, please fuck me' every time I see you. Eventually, I'm gon' do it because it breaks my heart to see you stressed like this and in so much pain."

Scorpio laughed and hit my arm with her purse. "I'm out of here. You done went too far, and trust me when I say that is not what I be thinking when I see you. Have fun with the kids, and I'll see you tomorrow morning."

She walked over to the kids to get at them. I couldn't help but to think how lucky I was. My relationship with Nokea and Scorpio was truly the best, especially since sex hadn't been a part of it. They both thought the grass was greener on the other side, so I put myself in a position to move out of the way so they could have at it. Thus far, it wasn't looking too good for either of them. What they were starting to realize was it really didn't get any better than this. That most men were untruthful and their issues were deeper than mine. That was my take on it, especially since they both shared with me the trials and tribulations of their new so-called relationships.

As I remained in thought, I looked up and saw Nokea coming outside, carrying a plate with two pieces of chicken on it. Before saying anything to me, she went over to the kids and Scorpio. They talked for a few minutes, and then Scorpio said goodbye to me again and left. Nokea came over and placed the plate next to me on the table. Her sweet perfume flowed through my nostrils. She was casually dressed in a short jacket, tight jeans, and high heels. Her short hair was spiked in the front and slicked down on the sides. My heart melted as I immediately thought about how the love of my life still resembled Nia Long. My love for both of them remained very strong.

"You haven't had a break from the kids since you've gotten home from Hell House," she said. "Would you like for me to take them to my place with me?"

"Nah, I'm good. We just chilling and relaxing, that's all. What's up with you?"

"I think I may hang out with Tiffanie tonight. She's been under a lot of stress regarding Shane, and if anyone can give her some advice about marriage, I guess it's me."

I didn't bite my tongue. "No offense, baby, but your advice about marriage sucks. You did kind of fuck up things around here, and I would think that you wouldn't want to pass on bad advice to Tiffanie."

Nokea's gaze rejected my comment. She knew I was playing with her, though, so she smiled. "I won't even comment on that mess you said, but I will say that I missed you while you were gone. I was thinking that we could maybe hang out tomorrow and go catch a movie. I also wanted you to see this new couch and bedroom set I'm thinking about purchasing. With your good taste, your opinion always matters."

"That may have to wait until I'm done with the Hell House reunion show. Then again, we don't necessarily hang out anymore, do we?"

She sat on the lounging chair next to me. "No, we don't, but we've become such great friends and loving parents. I'm kind of liking this little thing between us. How about you?"

"Like it? Nah, I love it. I love the fact that I'm here and you're almost ten miles away from me. I love that I don't have to know what the hell you're doing or who you're doing it with. And I love that I can sense when you want to get your fuck on, because you always come over here talking that 'hang out' bullshit. If making love is what you want to do, just say it."

She smiled and touched the side of my face. "Well, it's been a while, and I keep having these lip-licking, toe curling dreams about you that make me want to—"

I reached for her hand to stop her from teasing me. "Stop playing, baby. And whether you're being truthful or not, you know we don't get down like that, until you can be honest and tell me that you realize the grass is muddy on the other side and all you need is me. If not, we'll stay on this path—one that I'm perfectly fine with, so do you. I'll just continue to sit back and watch you from afar."

She knew what time it was. We'd had this discussion plenty of times before. She still didn't trust me; therefore, she didn't feel as though she wanted to fully commit herself to me again.

"Not even five minutes, Jaylin? You can't give me five measly minutes of your time?"

"I'm giving you five minutes right now. If you're talking about sexually, have you ever known me to give you five minutes? Within five minutes, all you gon' get is several licks on that pussy and minor finger action. I'm sure you want more than that, don't you?"

"I do, but it sounds like you're telling me to seek *comfort* elsewhere."

I placed my hands behind my head and shrugged. "Aye, I said it once and I'll say it again. Do what you gotta do, baby, and have fun while you're doing it. Make sure the brotha is strapped up, because I'm not down with getting any diseases when I decide to tamper with it again. Also, make sure he has good taste. It may help when you take him to see that furniture. I hope he can pay for it too. That way, you can stay the hell out of my pockets."

She leaned in to kiss my cheek. Then she stood and flaunted her perfect ass right in front of my face. I was saving something real special for her. Whenever I took the initiative to go there with her sexually, God help us both.

"Okay, Mr. Meanie, have it your way. I guess I'll see you when you get back from the reunion show. And whatever you do, please don't add another woman to your plate. In case you didn't know, it's already very full with someone special."

I winked at her with a smirk on my face. "No. In case you haven't noticed, my plate is empty. Sparkling clean, baby, and not one speck of a woman on it."

"Correction, sweetheart. As long as I still go by the name of Nokea Rogers, your plate will never be empty. I will always be somewhere on it, and that there is a fact."

She swished off, swaying with much confidence. I couldn't be mad at her. She definitely had her facts together, and there was no secret that I approved her message.

Talk about somebody who was happy that this was almost over with—that would be me. After Roc left the other day, I spoke to Jeff about how everything would go down. He gave me blow-by-blow details. First, he had to contact the others for the reunion show, and then he and his crew had to set up the backyard, where the show would take place. As far as the money, he was going to present me with the check for $100,000 during the reunion. Then I would be free to go.

Until then, I stayed in the house because my body was tired. That workout with Roc had done me in. I asked Jeff to bring me a cane so I could walk, and he brought me one yesterday. Meanwhile, I was pampered by a chef who Jeff brought in to cook for me and by a masseuse that hooked me up from head to toe yesterday. Jeff even had a stylist come in to tackle my hair. I loved the way she straightened it and parted it through the middle to fall on each side of my face. Now, it was time for her to show me what to wear. I wanted to look dope as ever, so I was counting on her to come through for me

The stylist, Karrine, had a gang of clothes piled on the bed. There were at least forty pairs of shoes in boxes, and the bling she showed me was off the chain. It looked very expensive; I suspected that some of the pieces cost a fortune. Jeff had gone all out for me. He also wanted to make sure I looked dynamite for the cameras. I was positive that whatever I chose to wear, I would look better than Sylvia and Chase put together.

"What about this?" Karrine said, as she held up a low-cut, dark-blue dress. "This is real sexy, isn't it?"

"It's sexy enough for me to wear when I'm layin' in my casket. I don't want to wear anything that dark. Next."

Karrine moved several of the elegant dresses aside. I didn't know why she brought all these after-five dresses. Many of them weren't my cup of tea or coffee.

"Okay. Now, you're going to like this. The color is popping, and with your skin tone, this will look spectacular on you."

I removed the orange dress from her hand, holding it in front of me. "I can work with this color, but I'm not tryin' to look like a fat pumpkin tonight. Don't you have somethin' for a plus-size, young diva with a great attitude? All this stuff you got here looks like it may be fittin' for an old lady. I got a long way to go before I get there, and please don't let this cane fool you."

Karrine sighed and laid the orange dress back on the bed. "All of these dresses are elegant and classy. They're not necessarily for older women, and younger women can wear them too. Why don't you pick out your favorite one and go try it on? I'm sure the dresses will look better on you than they do on these hangers."

I searched through more of the dresses and came across a yellow, baby-doll dress with one shoulder. It had beads across the top and tightened a bit around the waist. Before I made my way to the closet to change, Karrine found a pair of glittery, peep-toe heels to go with the dress.

"Try these on with the dress," she said with a smile. "They go perfect with it."

I wasn't sure why she was smiling so much, but I wanted to be sure about one thing, before we went any further. "I appreciate what you're doin' for me and everything, but you know I'm not payin' you, right? I don't have money to cover all of this."

Karrine threw her hand back at me. "It's already been taken care of. No worries. Just go and try on the dress."

"If I like it, do I get to keep it? Or do I have to return it tomorrow?"

"It's my understanding that you can keep everything. So choose as many of these dresses as you want, okay?"

I laid the cane on the bed and hurried into the closet. After I removed my clothes, I pulled the dress over my head. It was difficult to get it over my breasts and even harder to pull it past my stomach. I had to suck in several deep breaths before I was able to put the whole thing on to see how I looked.

Needless to say, I was hella disappointed. I looked a hot-ass mess in this dress. It lied to me while it was on that hanger looking good. Either that or I had picked up more weight than I thought I did. I had no waistline whatsoever, and the dress barely reached my knees. It was too damn short. When I turned around in the mirror, bending slightly over, I could see my peach panties. This was a no-no for me. I could see Jaylin and Prince laughing their asses off. Roc would lie and say that I looked decent, knowing damn well I didn't. Sylvia and Chase would be happy to see me in something like this. Just so they could whisper all night and talk mess behind my back.

"Let me see it," Karrine said, knocking on the door. "How does it look?"

"It looked fine on the hanger, but appears ridiculous on me. I'm done with this mess. You can save these dresses for somebody else. I'll find somethin' in this closet to wear."

She opened the door as I was trying to suck it in and pull the dress over my head. Yet again, it got stuck. This time, I started to kick up a sweat, trying to pull it off. She helped too. We struggled to pull the dress above my breasts.

"How did you get it on?" she asked. "And whatever you do, please don't tear it."

"Bitch, this dress is suffocatin' me and hurtin' my nipples. I'm about to pass the hell out. If I have to rip it to save my life, I will."

I pulled, she pulled, and we both pulled some more. After another minute, something had to be done.

"Would you go ask Jeff if he got some scissors? If not, you gon' have to do somethin' with that waistline. That's what's squeezin' my breasts."

"What if you push it down, over your hips? Let's try that first."

"Look at my ass, please. This dress ain't goin' over my hips or ass."

I'd had enough. My hair was getting messed up, and I didn't want it to sweat out before everybody got here. I backed away from Karrine and tussled with the dress, as if I was fighting to get it off me. I heard something rip. Whatever it was freed me.

"Darn it," Karrine said. "You ripped it."

A frown was clearly visible on my face. "So. It shouldn't have hurt me like that." Using the dress, I wiped sweat from my forehead and then tossed it to Karrine. "A needle and thread should take care of it. If not, I'm sure Jeff will. You can leave now. Thanks again for doin' my hair. Maybe I'll have better luck with those dresses next time."

Karrine left the closet with an attitude. By the time I came out of the closet, she had already taken some of the dresses to her van. This whole situation was embarrassing. It stressed me out. All I could do was sit at the kitchen table and eat chocolate ice cream with a disgusted look on my face.

"Do you need me to help you?" I said to Karrine, as she continued to make several trips from the bedroom to her van.

"No, thank you."

Her face was real twisted, but oh well. Had she brought some better choices over here, we wouldn't have had this problem. It wasn't my fault that she didn't have good taste.

By the time I finished my ice cream, Karrine was gone. I went back into the closet, choosing to wear my lime-green sweat suit and Nike tennis shoes. I felt like royalty in my outfit. This was much better than any of that bullshit Karrine brought over here.

Wasting more time, I sat on the couch and talked to Portia. We discussed what I would do with the money. I also discussed the same thing with Kenny. I figured I would kick both of them out a little something. Even though I had too many bills to pay, I would be able to help those in dire need.

Chase, however, didn't come across as if she was in dire need. We were supposed to split the money fifty-fifty, but since Jeff already told me that the check would be in my name, I wasn't so sure that I was going to up Chase's fifty percent. Maybe twenty-five percent. That was what her efforts were worth. I was the one who had to do the dirty work around here and make the call to eliminate Jaylin and Roc. It was hard as hell bringing them down. That didn't even include all the slaving in the kitchen I'd done. All Chase did was open her legs and call shots from afar. So, I wasn't feeling the whole fifty-fifty thing. Unfortunately, I hadn't gotten around to telling her why yet.

Time was flying by. I couldn't believe it was already 5:00 p.m. The reunion show wasn't going to start until six or six-thirty. I had already had dinner. The chef threw down on lobster and thin cuts of steak. He hooked up some buttered rolls and a pecan salad that made my mouth water. I had never eaten anything so tasty. Everything was seasoned to perfection. While he was in the kitchen cleaning up, I limped outside with the cane to look at the new setup of the backyard. Jeff and his crew had it laid out. There were six comfy lounging chairs with white linen padding, spaced out in a half circle. There was a slight chill in the air, so a covered fire pit sat several feet away from the chairs. Palms trees in humongous vases were propped up in several spaces, and the waterfall and rocks were used as a backdrop. A cocktail bar was to the far left and on top were numerous bottles of liquor for our drinking pleasures. It was apparent that Jeff was doing his best to create an inviting environment, especially for the cameras. Unfortunately, I suspected that many of the others wouldn't see this day as a celebration.

I went over to where Jeff and one of the cameramen were working. They were doing something with the lighting, but Jeff stopped to give me his attention.

"Do you need something, Jada?" he asked. "How's the back doing?"

"It's doin' okay. The cane is really helpin,' and thanks for bringin' it. I saw the bar over there and I wanted to be sure it was okay for me to get a drink."

"Sure. Help yourself. We should be done in about thirty more minutes. So far, what do you think?"

"It was already nice back here, but y'all done hooked it up even better. The palm trees done gave it a Hawaiian feel. I love it."

Jeff smiled and got back to work. I went over to the bar to get a drink. There was a tiny part of me that was kind of nervous because, even though I wanted to win, I didn't feel overly excited about the way things had went down with Jaylin and Roc. Even the incident with Prince was on my mind. Lord knows I didn't want to see him again. Then there was Sylvia. I had dissed her too. I was sure she'd have some words for me as well.

All of that was on my mind, in addition to the money. I had a hard time believing that I was about to get my hands on that kind of money. It had been a long time since I'd had access to a hundred g's. The last time I came close to money like that was when I was with Kiley. The drug money he had went a long, long way.

I poured Hennessy in a glass and hit it up with some ice. Right before I got ready to toss it back, the cell phone in my pocket rang. I looked at the phone and saw Chase's number on the screen.

I put the phone up to my ear. "Hello."

"Hey, what's up, chicka?"

"Nothin'. Just chillin' outside, watchin' Jeff and them set this whole thing up."

"How's it looking?"

"It's off the chain. I be glad when y'all get here 'cause my nerves are startin' to rattle."

"I know. I'm kind of nervous too, but think about where we'll be, once all of this is over. I'm going to take a vacation. I can already see the blue water and white, sandy beaches."

"I thought about taking a vacation too. I kind of want to do the Vegas thing with some of my friends, but not right away, though. I got some bills that I need to take care of before I do anything."

"I have a few that I need to knock out too, but not that many. I intend to spend my fifty thousand wisely. The money is what has me nervous, but I see a bright light at the end of the tunnel."

Her light was going to be a little dim once she found out I was only upping twenty-five thousand. Now wasn't the time to tell her. I probably wouldn't say anything until the check was in my hands.

"I'mma spend my portion wisely too, but hurry up and get here. I'm gettin' bored. Maybe my jitters will stop when you come."

"Okay, I'm coming. Let's just keep it cool tonight and try our best not to get into any confrontations. Smile away the anger and let no one get underneath your skin. As the winner, you know every-one is going to try to push your buttons. Don't let them, and please tell no one that we're splitting the money."

I looked up and had to take a double look when I saw Sylvia walk out the sliding glass doors. She was definitely trying to impress someone tonight. All I could do was roll my eyes at how cute she looked, especially with a gift in her hand. She placed it on a table that had a label marked "Gifts for Jada." I didn't make anything of it, because Jeff had already told me that he encouraged the others to bring gifts.

"Guess who just got here," I whispered to Chase.

"Who?"

"Sylvia."

"Really? Wha…what is she wearing?"

Sylvia stopped to spark up a conversation with Jeff, so I had a chance to thoroughly examine her attire.

"She got on a metallic-like dress that's cut above her knees. It got thin straps on it and it looks like she got on some of those glittery, red-bottom shoes. Her hair pent up, but bangs are swerved across her forehead. She got on gold hoop earrings and a bunch of gold and silver bangles are on her wrist. She look like she done lost a little weight 'cause the bitch's body is bad. Other than that, she carryin' an assistant Coach purse—the one she got don't look real. You gon' have to bring your A game, if you want to compete with this heifer."

"Oh, you can bet I will. Let me get off this phone. I need to start getting ready. I'm surprised she's there so early."

"Me too, but she is."

Chase said goodbye and I put the cell phone in my pocket. I kind of stretched the truth about how spectacular Sylvia looked to make Chase jealous. Sylvia did look nice, though, but on a scale from one to ten, I'd give her a seven. Her stomach was a little pudgy. It could've been better secured if she had worn a girdle. I was just saying.

I didn't like to be fake with folks, but after chugging down the Hennessy, I inched my way over to where Sylvia was, to find out why she was so early. She spotted me coming her way and tucked her clutch purse underneath her arm. The fakest grin I had ever seen was plastered on her face.

"What's up, girlee? What happened to you? Why do you have that cane?" She appeared concerned and met me halfway. We gave each other a hug and then backed up.

"I hurt myself messin' around with Roc in the workout room."

"Sounds like fun, especially if it was worth it."

"Nah, I don't mean like that. I meant he had me doin' some exercisin' that I ain't ever done before. I think I pulled somethin'. I won't know what, until I get out of here and go to the doctor. As soon as this is over with, I'm goin' to the emergency room to see what's up."

"I'm surprised you haven't gone to see a doctor yet. It could be serious, Jada."

"Maybe so."

Not wanting to stay outside, I headed indoors. Sylvia followed. Her perfume was working my nostrils, but it smelled like strawberries, which was good. I had to admit that she looked even better, now that we were in more light.

"You look nice," I said.

"You look cute too," Sylvia complimented.

She sat on the couch and crossed her bare legs that looked as if they had been dipped in baby oil. Her mani and pedi looked freshly done, and if I didn't know any better, I would've thought that she had won the money.

"I love your hair." She touched my hair to see if it were all mine. "Who did that for you?"

"A stylist came in here to hook me up. She did a good job, didn't she?"

"An awesome job. If you have her number, make sure I get it before you leave."

"I don't have it, but you can ask Jeff. He got that info for sure."

"Okay, I will. And before I forget, congrats on winning. I'm glad it was you and not any of the others, especially Jaylin."

I figured she was still upset with Jaylin, and since we seemed to share a cordial conversation, I brought her up to speed on what had gone down since she'd left. Her mouth kept widening and pure jealousy was trapped in her eyes when I told her about Chase having sex with Jaylin and Roc.

"Are you kidding me? What a slut. There is no secret that I had sex with Jaylin, but who goes around screwing two men in one day?"

"Some women do, but I'm not one to judge. Either way, it happened. Chase packed her stuff and left right after that."

Sylvia stayed tuned in to the updates. When I asked why she came early, she admitted to being nervous too.

"I'm eager to get this over with. I figured if I came early, I'd get a chance to relax and talk to you. Jeff said you were still here. I wanted to let you know that I have no hard feelings, even though you voted for me to leave."

"No hard feelings here either. I had to do what was necessary. And I'm not tryin' to go there with you, but bein' nice to me will not get me to split any of my winnings with you."

Sylvia laughed and snapped her finger. "Darn it. I wish you would have said that to me sooner," she said in a playful manner. "If so, I would've kept my compliments to myself."

I released a hearty laugh, but I still didn't like Sylvia. She came across as being phony. For now, I had to bear with it, but my whole demeanor changed when I looked up and saw the almighty Prince with a gift in his hand. I was shocked. He was prepped out in sagging jeans, a purple and gray argyle cardigan sweater, and new, unlaced white Jordan's. A white cap was cocked to the side on his head and he peered at me and Sylvia from behind a pair of tinted shades. All he did was toss his head back and then he headed toward the backyard.

Sure that he'd known I'd won the challenge, I excused myself from my conversation with Sylvia and made my way outside. For one, I wanted to let Prince know that I did not fear him, and I also wanted to find out where he'd gotten the weed from.

While holding myself up with the cane, I moved the sliding glass door aside. I called out Prince's name as he placed the gift on the table and stood next to Jeff. He glided my way, chewing gum and narrowing his eyes.

"I just wanted to speak and ask if you could provide me with some information," I said, being polite.

Prince halted his steps and stood in front of me. He blew a big bubble with the gum, then put it back into his mouth and chewed.

"What is it?" His tone was nasty, but I paid it no mind.

"You left some weed here, and Roc and I did our thing with it. Can you let me know where you got it from, so I can hook myself up from time to time?"

Prince looked me over with his light-brown eyes. He blew another bubble, then let out a soft snicker before turning to walk away from me.

"Damn, it's like that," I said. "You too bitter to let me know where you got yo weed from?"

With his back turned, he held up his middle finger. It wasn't that I had expected the ol' Cracker Barrel-eating nigga to be my best friend, I was only asking about his weed connection. I tried not to get upset, but he rubbed me the wrong way.

"Fuck you too, Prince. If you want to continue this beef when we get up out of here, we can."

He swung around and grabbed his manhood. "Bitch, I ain't got time for you right now. Go sit down somewhere or suck on this to keep yo mouth shut."

Jeff and his crew members were already on alert. All I did was laugh at Prince, knowing that it would anger him more. "Boy, please. Don't nobody want to suck on yo STD-infected dick." I looked at Jeff. "Be sure to pat that idiot down, Jeff, 'cause if he lay one hand on me today, you gon' be carrying him out of here in a body bag."

Jeff had high hopes for the reunion show, so you best believe that he tried to calm things down. He pulled Prince aside to talk to him. I, on the other hand, limped back inside and damn near fainted when I spotted Roc sitting on the couch next to Sylvia. Almost immediately, the sparkling diamond in his earlobe hit me first. His dark-chocolate skin appeared smooth as soft leather and his facial hair was sharply trimmed to pure perfection. The deep-red, V-neck Polo sweater he rocked rested on his broad shoulders and bulging biceps. The color looked dynamite against his dark skin and his baggy Levi's had the meat between his legs sitting pretty. After being inside of this house with Roc for so long, I guess I'd forgotten how well he cleaned up. Seeing him made my heart skip several beats. I now regretted not having sex with him when I had the chance. Damn!

I predicted that he was still swoll, but he did have a gift on his lap. I went into the living room and took a seat on the far right side of the couch. As expected, Roc didn't even look my way. Sylvia's fake self was putting it on thick. I wondered if she had been visualizing her legs thrown over his shoulders like I saw mine.

"I'm glad it is too," she said, responding to whatever Roc had said. "Meanwhile, I need to go to the bathroom. Excuse me for a minute."

She wiggled her hips and pulled on her dress that had hiked up a bit. Then she stepped over Roc, and you'd better believe that his eyes were glued to her ass like superglue. As much trouble as his tail was in, he should've shielded his eyes or looked in another direction. Instead, his eyes followed her until she went into the bathroom. My hope was that she took care of the problem with her pudgy stomach. Her belly looked full. If she was going to wear a dress like that, her stomach needed to be flat as a board. I started to take off my girdle and give it to her, but I wanted her to keep on flouncing around here like she was all that. I laughed to myself at my jealousy. As long as my thoughts weren't spoken out loud, I was good.

Roc must've gotten tired of being in my presence. He got up and walked away. All I got was a whiff of his cologne. Not too many black men were doing it like he was. How he ever found a pair of jeans that fit his ass and thighs so perfectly, I didn't know. Desa Rae had her hands full with him. I wished that I still had that flash drive so I could watch him in action. I reminded myself to ask Chase if she had another one.

Sylvia came out of the bathroom, rushing as if she had lost something.

"Where did Roc go?" she asked in a whisper.

"He went outside. I guess to get away from me."

She stepped further into the room, but she didn't sit down. "Did you see how fine that man was? Talk about sexy, wow."

I rolled my eyes, hoping that she didn't notice. "Of course I saw him. He cleans up real well, but—"

Just then, we heard shoes hit the hardwood floors. Our eyes shifted to the hallway, and seconds later, Jaylin appeared in the flesh. Before I could even describe what my eyes had witnessed, I saw Sylvia hold her breath, back up, and slowly ease down on the couch. These black folks up in here weren't playing. They treated this shit like it was a red carpet event. Unfortunately, I was the only one underdressed. I'll be damned if Jaylin didn't have us squirming around like slithering snakes. He was without a smile and without a gift. But that serious gaze he carried in his eyes was enough to make a bitch drop her panties without him saying a word. And the suit…Lord have mercy. The black tailored suit he wore was cut to fit every detail of his athletic frame. The color from his soft, powder-blue silk shirt reflected off his super-rich grey eyes that sat behind his long lashes. His thinly trimmed goatee squared perfectly around his mouth and chin, but his healthy, curly hair classified his overall appearance as one-in-a-million. Sylvia and me both were hypno-tized by his presence, and as he stepped further into the room, his jewelry was blinding. Particularly, the diamond watch on his wrist that probably cost every bit of the hundred thousand dollars I was about to win. Everything about him said fucking fabulous and his persona was that of a well-established man.

"Is anybody gon' speak?" he asked.

Sylvia's ol' dumb self still hadn't moved. Her eyes were without a blink. I was hoping that Jaylin snapped his finger to snap her out of her trance. I kept glaring at his smooth, tanned skin, but I came back to life when I felt a jab in my pussy. *Eaaaasy,* I thought. *Calm down, cooda, you gone get some one day. Hopefully.*

I surely didn't want Jaylin to know what his looks were doing to me, so I patted my chest and cleared the clogged mucus from my throat.

"Hi. Mostly everybody is here, but they're outside."

That was all I could say and could say no more. He pulled his suit jacket back and slipped his hand into his pocket. The black leather belt around his waist held up his pants, and I could see how well his neatly tucked-in shirt ripped across his chest and abs. Sylvia's eyes lowered to the bulge in his pants. I felt for whatever she was going through. Her eyes appeared watered and she inched up from her seat.

"Excuse me for being rude," she said. "But I need to go."

She hurried out of the room to go outside. Jaylin shrugged, and then he looked at me.

"Nice do," he said, referring to my hair. "And congrats on your win."

"Thank you," I replied in a soft tone, still a bit choked up by his presence.

There was so much more that I wanted to say to him, but unfortunately, my body wasn't cooperating. I stood and then told Jaylin that I had to use the bathroom. He strutted outside, and I let the cane drop to the floor and rushed to the bathroom, closing the door behind me. I turned on the faucet to splash my face with cold water. Once that was cool, I yanked my sweatpants and panties down to my ankles and unrolled a bunch of toilet paper around my hand. I then hiked up my leg on the toilet and wiped the excitement that was building between my legs. Seeing Jaylin had me hotter than four hoes at an election rally waiting for Obama to speak. I was that hot. At that moment, I realized what a fool I'd been for not getting some kind of pleasure from Jaylin or Roc. At least Sylvia and Chase had life-long memories to take with them.

All I had was a wet coochie that was mad as hell at me and nowhere near satisfied. I wasn't sure how this reunion show was going to turn out, but since Jaylin was speaking to me, I was sure to be on my best behavior, just in case he wanted to delve into something a little later.

Five minutes later, I was good to go. I picked up my cane that I'd thrown on the floor and inched my way into the backyard. I could see that everyone had taken their seats. Sylvia had the nerve to take a seat between Jaylin and Roc, and Prince was on the other side of him. There was an empty chair next to Jaylin and an empty chair beside that chair. Since Chase hadn't made it yet, I hurried, as fast as I could to take the seat next to him. I was surprised that Chase hadn't gotten here yet. When I looked at the clock, it was almost six-thirty.

Small talk was happening within our half circle and most of the conversation was between Roc and Sylvia. Jaylin and Prince exchanged a few words, but I kept looking around at Jeff and his crew as they put the finishing touches on the backyard.

"What happened to you?" Jaylin asked, looking at the cane beside me.

"I hurt myself in the workout room. I was tryin' to make you proud of me and I wanted to lose about ten pounds before you came back here."

"Don't do anything for me. Do it for yourself. And I told you what you needed to do to lose weight, but you refused to listen."

"Well, Roc said I needed to work out in the gym. His body is way more tight than yours is, so I took his advice instead of yours."

Jaylin tried to ignore my comment. He asked if I had anything to drink. "Maybe that's why you seem a little confused," he said.

"I already had some Hennessy, but I'm about to get up and get another glass. Would you like for me to get you somethin'?"

"I can get it. Don't want you walking around a lot and hurting yourself even more."

I stood and reached for the cane. "I'm good. Besides, the more I move around, the better I feel."

"I bet. Please pour me some Remy in a sparkling clean glass, no ice."

It was the least I could do for Jaylin, considering I had voted to have him kicked out of the house. I didn't even trip off his sparkling clean glass comment, because I had gotten to know his anal self pretty well by now. I wanted to inquire about the flash drive, but I assumed that if he wanted to talk about it, he would bring it up later.

I got up to get our drinks, but as soon as I heard Prince's voice, I turned around.

"Ooooo-weee," he said, looking toward the sliding doors. "Daaa-aamn, ma, you doin' it like that!"

Everybody's eyes were focused in the same direction. I followed suit and saw Chase from afar. She stopped to hug Jeff and was conversing with him and several of his crew members. I'll just say that if I were a lesbian, I'd have that bitch's legs cocked open right now. Her late appearance had Roc biting down on his lip, Sylvia rolling her eyes, and Jaylin softly stroking his goatee. Prince's words said enough.

Chase had not only shown up, but she showed out. The peach, sheer and sleeveless mini-dress she wore put shame to the word sexy. Decorative nude-colored flowers that were printed on the dress hid some of her private parts, but the sheer parts of the dress didn't leave much to the imagination. Parts of it revealed her perky breasts and curvy hips. She didn't have on a stitch of underclothes and her nude, peep-toe pumps blended in well with her caramel skin. Every strand of her hair was pulled back into a sleek ponytail—I wondered how much sperm was needed to pull that off—but her hair was pulled back so tightly that it made her hazel eyes slant. Her high brows were arched and the rose-colored makeup she wore dazzled everyone. She put her gift for me on the table, and as she hugged Jeff, he didn't seem to want to let go. She shot him a wink, knowing that she had the attention on lock. I had no idea what her dress revealed from the backside, but as Jeff and his entire crew's eyes were on her, I could only imagine what they saw when she walked away. She worked the pathway up to us like a professional model on the runway. We all kept staring, and as soon as I gave Jaylin his drink, I hurried to return to my seat.

By then, Sylvia's head was turned in another direction, Roc was pretending to look at a text message on his phone, Prince was still acting thirsty, and Jaylin looked straight ahead with a blank expression on his face. Chase proceeded our way, shifting her eyes from Roc to Jaylin. She stared him down without a blink. I was positive that she would have to make a bathroom run like I did later. She walked up and stood right in front of me.

"Jada, would you please move over. I want to sit next to Jaylin, if you don't mind."

This bitch was tripping if she thought I was fixing to get up out of my chair, so she could sit next to Jaylin. Before I could say anything, I could see Prince leaning to the side with his mouth dropped open as he checked out Chase's backside.

"Damn, shorty, you can sit right here if you want to," he said, patting his lap. "I had no idea you were workin' with all of that."

Chase turned her head to the side, blushing as she looked at Prince. "Thanks for the compliment, Prince, and hello, Roc, Sylvia, and Jaylin." Her eyes shifted from one person to the next. Sylvia was the only one to speak back, aside from Prince who had already welcomed her. Jaylin did so with a nod, but Roc said not one word. As for me, I pointed to the chair next to me.

"That's your seat. I saved it for you."

Chase narrowed her eyes and gave me an evil stare. But she kept a fake grin on her face. She moved from in front of me, and instead of taking a seat, she sashayed over to the bar. Why? Because she knew damn well that all heads would turn in the same direction. They did, and she took her time preparing a drink. The back of her mini-dress was as sexy as the front. The flowers started from the top of her left shoulder and flowed down her back like an S shape that covered only a portion of her ass. I didn't remember it being that big, but if she had gotten some ass injections, it was her business, not mine. Her perfect waistline could be seen through the sheer and so could a portion of her butt cheeks. I felt like running into the house to change clothes, and I now regretted not choosing one of the dresses the stylist had shown me. Chase had outdone herself. I had to admit that she impressed the hell out of me. I was so impressed that I let her take my seat, next to Jaylin. She thanked me and then sat down and crossed one leg over the other. Her posture was perfect, and she poked out her breasts to make them appear larger. After sipping from her glass, she shot a seductive look at Jeff and smiled.

"Ready whenever you are," she said to him. "And please forgive me for being tardy for the party."

I was sure that Jeff wouldn't hold it against her, but like it or not, it was time to get this show on the road.

Sylvia

I couldn't wait for this day to come. I had so much on my mind that I needed to say. Not even Jonathan's good sex the other day could calm my nerves, and I was kind of on edge because I hadn't heard from him. Now that I was here, I was feeling some kind of way about it. Based on what Jada had told me about what had happened after I left, I felt even more livid with Jaylin for being such a womanizer. I had a chance to see him and tell him what had been on my mind, but it was so funny that I changed my mind about saying anything, particularly about his conversation with Jonathan. The plan was to let Jaylin know how I felt about his disrespect and to acknowledge that, even though what he'd said to me was the truth, it still hurt. I was the one who should've known better. It was so unlike me to throw myself at a man like that, and I'd already had a bad reputation for falling for my best friend's husband. I used these several weeks away from Hell House to reevaluate my actions. I promised myself that I'd start making better choices. But now that I knew Jaylin had screwed Chase, the only thing that I was going to acknowledge was what a dog I thought he was.

Jeff said that he'd be ready to go in a few more minutes. I was happy to be sitting next to Roc. He offered good conversation. We laughed and discussed some of the ups and downs during our stay in the house. Our conversation halted when Chase arrived. The men watched her like she was prey. I could tell that Roc wasn't that moved by her presence because of the tightness of his face. The closer she got to us, he cut his eyes and looked away. To me, I thought she looked decent, but the dress she wore was too revealing. It gave her an official slut title. I guess she was trying to pull off a look only Jennifer Lopez or Halle Berry could do on the red carpet. But Chase had failed miserably. I wasn't trying to hate, but nobody cared to see her private parts peeking at them, did they? Then again, maybe so, because lust was on display as well as shock.

Jada seemed surprised by what Chase had on too. And speaking of Jada, the sweat suit she wore was not fit for the occasion. This wasn't a picnic. Didn't she know this was being filmed? There was no telling who would be watching. Her hair was beautiful, though. All in all, she was a chubby, cute woman with an obscenely foul mouth that was irritating.

All of the men brought their A game. I'd gotten used to seeing them dressed in basketball shorts, wife beaters, and T-shirts. There were days when their hair was not so fresh, beards were a bit rugged, but today made up for it all. While I was sure that I wouldn't see either of them again, my intentions were to make the best of this day and leave here with no regrets.

Jeff still wasn't ready, so I got up to get a drink. Roc and Prince were having a conversation about cars and Jada and Chase were chatting like best friends. Jaylin was talking to someone on his cell phone. His words implied that it was about business. I strutted by him, hoping that he would look up. He did so, but the blank expression that he'd had thus far was locked there. Jada and Chase stopped talking, but I heard Jada say something like, "suck it in."

"Suck what in?" I stopped to ask.

"Nothin'. I was just speakin' out loud to myself."

I shrugged and kept it moving. At the bar, I poured a glass of sparkling champagne, then returned to my seat. Roc reached out his hand.

"Where's mine at?" he asked.

"I didn't know you wanted anything. You should have said something."

"Nah, I'm good. I was just messin' with you."

There was a part of me that wished I had gotten with him instead of Jaylin. Roc seemed so down to earth, respectful, funny, and non-judgmental. The fact that he'd mentioned his woman caused me to back away, but apparently his woman didn't matter if he and Chase had had sex.

While I was drinking my champagne, Jeff pulled up a lounging chair that sat on the other side of the fire pit. His chair faced us, and it looked as if he was ready to start. Casually dressed in a polo shirt, khaki pants with a heavy crease, and brown leather loafers, he took a seat. His eyes searched from Jada to Prince and he grinned at all of us.

"Good evening," he said. "Thanks to all of you for being here. It's time to get started. Before we do, I ask that all cell phones are turned off and put away. I also ask that you respect others in here by not over talking and being rude. As most of you already know, Jada Mahoney is the winner of this challenge. At the very end of the reunion show, I will present her with a check for one hundred thousand dollars. Before we get started, are there any questions or concerns for me?"

Jaylin spoke up first. "No questions now, but I'll damn sure have some for you later."

Jeff nodded. "Jaylin, I welcome any questions that you have. I'll be happy to answer them, whenever the time comes."

Jada smacked her lips. "My questions are, why do I have to wait until later to get my check? And are we supposed to just sit here and look at each other or what? I mean, how is all of this supposed to go down?"

"It was my decision to give the check to you later. How this will go down is I'll ask questions for each of you to answer. Some of the questions are from people who have gotten to know all of you rather well. You'll have an opportunity to express anything that's on your mind, and once you're done, everyone will be free to go home."

"How long will this bullshit take?" Roc said. He had much built-up anger inside of him. I wondered why.

"Hopefully, not too long. Maybe an hour or two, if that."

"You ain't said nothin' but a word. Proceed."

Jeff gave no reply. He looked to his left where Jada was sitting with a drink in her hand.

"Jada, I'm going to go around the room, and starting with you, tell us what you've learned from this experience. What advice would you offer the other people here, based on how you feel they live their everyday lives? Your experience in Hell House should've enabled you to offer valuable input."

Jada sat silent for a minute and then sighed. I assumed her mind was racing like mine was.

"You may want to start somewhere else," she said. "Cause some people might not like what I have to say. I don't want to offend anyone or hurt their feelings."

She gave Prince an evil-eye as he cracked his knuckles.

"We're all adults here," Jeff said. "Everyone should be able to handle what you have to say. If they can't, that's their problem, not yours."

"You got that shit right," Jada said with a spark of enthusiasm. She turned to her left, clearing her throat before speaking. "Chase, you my girl and everything, but I think you are totally screwed up in the head. You be actin' real thirsty sometimes, and a woman who got it goin' on like you don't need to conduct yourself that way. Plus, you real bossy. You think people should always do what you say, but we grown up in here. Ain't nobody gotta listen to you. You need to chill with that. You also need to learn how to cook. I mean, pussy don't always keep a man on lock. You gotta know how to put something good in his belly. My suggestion would be for you to take some cooking classes and stop chasing men until you learn how to satisfy them one hundred."

Chase put on a fake smile, pretending as if what Jada said didn't sting. Truthfully, she'd nailed it. I couldn't have said it any better. Jada continued when she moved her eyes over to Jaylin.

"I learned a lot about men from you, Jaylin, and there ain't no question that you made my stay here hella fun. My only gripe with you is yo anal behavior. You need to know that yo cleanliness was a pain in the ass and some of us black folk don't get down with the cleanin' like you do. My advice would be for you to never come to my house, because a few cockroaches do reside there. I'mma also need for you to see an anger management counselor. You got some anger issues that need to be resolved. Sylvia, unfortunately, I'mma have to hurt yo feelings 'cause I think you are fake as all outdoors. You bring negative energy into the room and you need special education classes on how to keep it real. Truth is, I really don't like you, but since you ain't payin' my bills, I don't have nothin' else to say."

I couldn't help but to respond. "And I don't like you either. You're full of crap, Jada, and you're so wrong about me and—"

Jeff interrupted. "Please, Sylvia, remain quiet. You'll have your opportunity to respond. Allow her to finish."

I rolled my eyes and tapped my heel on the ground. I couldn't wait to have my say. Thankfully, Jada moved on.

"Roc, I love you too, boo, and even though you mad at me, you need to cut back on the weed and get yo life in order. If you want to profess love for somebody, stand up and be the man yo lady needs you to be. Stop runnin' around teasin' folks, and makin' promises that you ain't gon' keep. Lastly, keep yo dick in yo pants. There are too many chicks who would take the risk of ridin' on it, but if you ain't on the market, man up and say that shit. Prince, I'm not gon' tell you how I feel about you because you already know. I will say one thing and that is your home trainin' ain't worth a damn. Yo Mama or Daddy done failed you. With a li'l hope and change, maybe you'll do better."

Prince was hyped about her comments like I was. His face twisted and he held up his middle finger the whole time Jada talked to him. "I accept no advice from a fat, ghetto, low-life bitch who don't know—"

"Prince, please," Jeff said. "We have to cut the interruptions and allow everyone to speak what is on their minds."

"Finish, slut," he said to Jada. "I'm listenin'."

"Yo dookey-breath Mama, bastard," Jada said, rolling her eyes. "But anyway, what I learned from this experience is some women need to learn how to cook, especially if they want to keep a man, and some men need to stop usin' they dicks to get what they want. Livin' in a house with five other black people is fucked up. I would never want to do this again."

Jada looked at Jeff. He thanked her for being honest. Prince and I appeared to be the only two highly upset by Jada's comments. I guess the others knew how to control themselves. Chase was next, but instead of sitting to say what was on her mind, she stood up. She crossed her arms, starting with Jada.

"I won't respond to your statement about me being thirsty, and I reject every word you said about me; it doesn't apply. You, however, have no class whatsoever. I encourage you to return to school to further your education, because you come across as a real dumb-ass trick. Pertaining to food, girl, hook up with a dietitian and be done with it. You could stand to lose some serious weight and your goal should be looking like me. That's hard to do, but the least you can do is try."

Prince slapped his leg and started cracking up. "You got that shit right!" he shouted.

"Sit your triflin' self down somewhere, before I knock you upside your head with this cane," Jada said to Chase. "You the one who ain't got no class. A bitch with two dicks in her in one night ain't got no room to talk. I'm one hundred percent satisfied with the way I look, thank you very much. And when you get done talkin', any decent man would take a curvy *trick* like me any day, over a skank who can't even make a grilled cheese sandwich."

Roc snickered, Jaylin sighed, and Prince held his hand inches away from his mouth. "Damn, for real?" he said. "Chase did it like that with two dicks? Fuck, I missed out!"

Jeff yelled for silence, but Jada seemed highly upset. "Don't get me started. I tried to be cordal, but you went off on the deep end with me. If I add Jeff to the mix, then you really gon' have to sit down and clamp yo mouth shut."

All eyes shifted to Jeff. Hell, what about him? Did Chase have sex with him too? Oh, my. I wanted to know the scoop. Apparently, everybody else did as well. Jeff jumped up from his chair and put his hands in his pockets. "Jada, the word is cordial, not cordal. If you continue to interrupt, I'll have to ask you to leave and give someone else the money. Please remain calm, and Chase, be careful with your comments."

Chase softened her tone, but tried to make her point. "You asked us to say what was on our minds. I was only keeping it real. I make no apologies for it, and if Jada didn't like what I had to say, I'm sorry, too bad. Moving on," she said, turning to Jaylin with glee in her eyes. He appeared nonchalant, while looking straight ahead. "I don't have anything, not one single negative thing to say about you, and on a positive note, you are ridiculously handsome. It was a pleasure spending time with you, and I consider myself so lucky for having the opportunity to get to know you on another level. My hope is that our friendship can continue."

"Ugh," Jada said, frowning. "I want to throw up. Stop ridin' so doggone much."

"Please," I added. "Move on."

Chase's words were sickening. The last thing she needed to do was act as if Jaylin was all that. Obviously, she was trying to hook up with him again. He had the audacity to thank her for the "kind" words.

"Before I continue," Chase said. "I'm going to need both of you bitches to stop hating. She looked from Jada to me, but neither of us said a word.

"Proceed," Jeff said. "Without any more interruptions."

Chase gawked at me with deviousness in her eyes. "I ditto what Jada said about you, Sylvia, but I'm going to add much more to it. You are a phony woman who will get no high praises from me.

You don't come across as being a loyal person, and I'm sure you'll find yourself all alone one day, without any friends. There is not one single thing that I like about you, and when it comes to men, my hope is that you learned a little something from me. Your approach is tired and played out. I don't blame Jaylin for dissing you, and that's what you get for presenting him with a weak game."

"I learned… Not. One. Thing," I said. "And I don't take advice from whores who open their legs and mouths to numerous men who use them."

All Chase did was chuckle. I swallowed hard. My feelings were bruised. It was difficult to hear one person say something negative about me, but when two people said the same thing, it stung. Jada or Chase didn't know much about me, but the loyal thing got to me because of what I had done to someone I considered a best friend. I pretended not to trip and listened to Chase express herself to Roc. He sat with his elbows resting on his knees, staring like he wanted to kill her.

"The truth is, I don't have a beef with you, so please calm down and stop looking at me like that. Don't be upset with me because you made the wrong choices. What woman wouldn't pursue you, Roc; after all, you are a very attractive man. Out of all of us, you should've learned the most. You can't play around with love, and you need to be careful about who you slide your thing into. I'll leave it there after I remind you of the dire consequences of trying to have your cake and eat it too. Prince, you got a bad wrap up in here. I like you, a lot, but stop trying to be so hard. Never resort to putting your hands on a woman. Learn to walk away from fools who push you into confrontations and then cry out as victims. I'm sure you know what I mean."

Prince nodded, evidently feeling what Chase had said.

"Is she referrin' to me as the foolish victim?" Jada said, but was ignored. "Okay, I'mma show that ass who the fool is. Watch."

"What I've learned from this experience is some women will always be the catty, backstabbing, jealous, and hating bitches who they are. Sexy men can always get it, and I will never do this again, unless Jaylin is in the same house with me."

Chase glanced at Jaylin, but he didn't respond. He looked to be in deep thought. That round left Jada sitting in her chair fuming and me wanting to walk the hell out. I was two-for-two in the negative.

"Jaylin," Jeff said. "We're ready whenever you are."

"I don't think it's appropriate to sit here and tell people things they already know about themselves. It really ain't my place to judge or bring a bunch of bullshit to their attention. But I have no problem playing by the rules, and just so everybody here knows, any and all negative or positive comments addressed to me will go in one ear and out the other. I'm well aware of my issues, but I'm one hundred percent happy with who I am. I suspect that no one here can advise me on how to increase my net worth, so feel free to skip over me, unless, of course, you have proven credentials that can qualify you as being my financial advisor. With that, Jada knows she's out there and her vocabulary is fucked up. Chase is sexy as fuck, but use the pussy for other things, other than playing on brotha's minds." Jaylin finally looked up and turned in her direction. "For the record, revenge always backfires. You know what I'm talking about, so think before you act, all right?"

Chase had nothing to say, causing Jaylin to turn his head to me. "Sylvia, you know how I feel, because I already told you. The best thing you can do is direct your anger toward the man who really hurt you. That man is not me, so stop living that lie. Roc, reconsider the marriage thing. You're young, and a man in his twenties needs not to commit unless his mind is mature enough to do so. When you're ready, you'll know it. Prince, I feel for you, but parental direction or not, know better and do better. This experience has shown me that there are way more fucked up people in this world than me. Money remains the root of all evil, and it will remain limited to those who stab others in their backs to get it. Be careful who you step on in the process, because you never know when your greed may come back to bite and take a chunk out of yo ass. If given the opportunity, I would definitely do this again. It has benefited me in every single way possible."

Silence soaked the backyard. Jaylin's words didn't hurt me as much as Jada's and Chase's did, but Chase was the one, out of all of us, who seemed taken aback. It was my turn. I had hoped to keep my cool, but as soon as I opened my mouth, my words turned harsh.

"Jada, you need to be in a mental institution, instead of Hell House. You're an embarrassment to African American women, and my wish is for you to return to school and study English."

"And my wish is for you to purchase a high-priced girdle that can suck in your sloppy stomach that is makin' yo dress look awful. How's that for bein' an embarrassment to black women? You do none of us any justice by walkin' around here with a potbelly in a mini-dress. What exactly was you thinkin', you messy hooka? I'm confused."

"That you are. Very confused, so be sure to handle that."

I figured Jada wouldn't like what I had to say. If that was all she could use to attack me, I happily ignored her.

"Chase, you're trash. You appear to be one of those women who make a living chasing dick to fill a void that no dick will repair. I feel sorry for you the most because you're used up and don't even know it. No man will ever take you seriously until you wise up and face your demons. There appears to be a lot of them. Tackle whatever it is that makes you resort to being such a slut and good luck on your transition to becoming a better woman."

Jada busted out laughing. "Hell, naw. She done went the fuck off! Call it as you see it, ho, I'm listenin'.'"

Chase jerked her head to the side and cut her eyes at Jada. She then stood and pointed her finger at me. "If I didn't call you any names, then I want the same respect in return. How dare you call me a slut when you opened your legs, invited Jaylin into his friend's pussy the first night you were here, and then cried about it when you got dissed? I—"

I turned to Jeff, asking that he speak up to silence her as he had done everyone else. "Let Sylvia finish, Chase," he said. "She deserves a turn too."

"Thank you," I said, watching as Chase sat back down and clamped her mouth shut. Her brows were raised and she was mad as hell. Great.

My moment of truth was now here. I sucked in a deep breath and then released it. "Jaylin, the real reason I'm here is because of you. I'm not going to stroke your ego, as some of us have clearly already done, but here are the facts. All you do is trample on the hearts of women. You don't give a damn about nobody but yourself. You use your good looks, charm, and money to entice women, and when they begin to express their love for you, you take advantage of that love or treat love as if it's a crime. You may very well be satisfied and happy with who you are; good for you. I, however, see you as a slick, dog-ass, trifling, motherfucking Negro who will eventually get what is coming to you. When that day comes, I hope that whoever the lucky woman is, I hope that she rips your heart from your chest and stomps on it. My wish is that she delivers enough pain to you, in return for all of the pain I'm sure you have dished out for many years. From the outside, you may be one of the most gorgeous men I have ever laid my eyes on, no doubt. But your insides are rotten and uglier than that bitch sitting next to you. That would be Chase."

Chase shot up from her chair and clapped her hands. All Jaylin did was nod and rub the hairs on his chin.

"Finally," Chase said still clapping. "The fake ho is gone and the real foul-mouth tramp has shown up. I knew you could do it, Sylvia. Thank you for throwing away the mask so we could all get a glimpse of the real you."

"You're welcome. Now, sit your trashy tail down so I can finish."

Jada couldn't control herself. She was laughing and clapping so loudly that her claps were echoing. "Preach! I swear y'all hoes are messy," she shouted. "But I want exactly what you're havin', Sylvia. Is it by chance a V-8 or some Vitamin Water?"

"Please stop all that yelling in my ear," Chase shouted to Jada. "It's not that serious."

"If you don't like it, move. And it is that serious, because Miss Fakety-Fake done awakened from the dead and called out some people on their shit."

Jeff had to remind us again to stay quiet and remain respectful. I was able to continue after Chase and Jada got finished exchanging a few more unkind words. Jaylin had also expressed that he was happy I had gotten that off my chest.

"I'm glad that I did too. Roc and Prince, I have no words. I wish the two of you the best, and Roc, in the future, please be able to decipher trash from treasure. Good luck to you and Desa Rae. I hope everything works out for you."

He reached out to shake my hand. "Thanks, ma. The best to you too."

Prince saluted me.

"There is nothing anyone can say or do to make me relive this Hell House experience again," I said. "And while it has been quite a learning experience, I prefer to forget about all that has happened here and move on."

I was done and needed to say no more. Roc was up. It didn't appear that he was going to hold back either. He stood in front of Chase and Jada, displaying a whole lot aggression. So much so that two of the bodyguards moved in closer to him.

"Ain't no need to get that close to me," Roc said to the bodyguards. "I'm just speakin' my piece as I was asked to do. Don't allow the color of my skin to shake y'all up."

The white bodyguards backed up, but Jada and Chase sat like two school girls with attitudes locked on their faces.

"Listen up, Thelma and Louise," Roc said. "I don't know the details of the game y'all playin' here, but here's what's up. There are certain things that happened here that needs to stay here. Jada, take your paper and go live happily ever after. Do not speak my name again, and better yet, you don't know me and I don't know you. Chase, the same goes for you. If you think I'm some robotic nigga that you gon' toy and play games with, you got me fucked up. Whatever plans y'all got needs to be reprocessed and squashed. If not, y'all have my word that if any of this noise comes to my doorstep or travels through the ears of the woman on my team, there will be some dirt layin' and all-night prayin' goin' on by your family and friends who will miss you. This is no threat, only a promise. If you bold, try me. If you feel what I'm sayin', good luck and good riddance."

He slammed his hand against Jaylin's, he kissed me on the cheek, then he gave Prince dap too.

"Holla at me about that weed," he said to Prince. "Don't forget."

He walked off and moved toward Jeff.

"Where are you going?" Jeff asked him. "We're not done yet."

"You may not be, but I am. I'm gettin' the fuck out of here. Got matters to tend to at home. This shit done already took up too much of my time."

"You can't leave yet," Jeff said. "We have a contract that—"

Roc's voice went up a notch. "To hell with that contract. I don't give a damn. Sue me."

He strutted toward the exit. Jeff flipped through several index cards in his hand and yelled out to Roc. "Wait one minute! Please answer one question. It's from Krisha in Detroit."

Roc halted his steps and turned around.

"Krisha says that she's had some fire weed before, and although she was higher than a Giraffe's pussy, the weed never clouded her judgment to the point where she would mess up her situation at home. She wants to know if you were really that high when you had sex with Chase or did you want to get it because Chase was willing to pop her coochie on you from the jump?"

We were all tuned in to Roc's reply, especially Chase, who had moved to the edge of her seat.

"Of course I was fucked up," Roc said. "But Krisha is right. Weed ain't ever made me do anything that I didn't want to do. I don't succumb to pressure either, and the only reason my dick entered Chase was because I wanted it to. She played on my intelligence and I tripped. The real woman I got at home shouldn't have to share my dick, especially not with a bitch on Chase's level. My bad, so now I got to shake up some things with Black Love and hope that everything works out for me. Peace again, I'm out."

He walked out. Sadly, it was the last that I would ever see of him. Then again, who knows?

There was no secret that almost everyone sitting here had me fired up. I wanted to punch Jada in her face, but no more than I wanted to slap Sylvia and run after Roc to beat him down. He really upset me. Now, he had me more eager to let Desa Rae know that I was her sister; the one he had screwed. I wasn't the least bit afraid of his threats. All they did was motivate me. He had no idea that this thing was much deeper than him, and it was now my chance to seek revenge against the one sister my father had always compared me to; the one who he considered his "Angel," while I was nothing but a hole for him to stick his dick into. My day was coming. So was Roc's.

As for Jaylin, he was on point with some of the words he'd spoken, but like him, what I didn't want to hear went in one ear and out of the other. I was going to continue on doing me, and there was nothing no one could do about it.

Prince was the last one to speak on his experience and offer advice. After Roc flew out of here like a coward, we all listened to Prince.

"I refuse to tackle y'all one by one in detail, but I'll say my piece on an overall basis. Dittoin' what Jaylin said, we all fucked up, so why or how do y'all feel as though it's okay to point the finger at the next man and tell them what they need to fix? I know what's up with me, and while I'm nowhere near one hundred, I will say that I am a better man than I was the day before. Nobody here has taken the same journey as me, so don't try to dictate how I need to go about doin' things. I try to make my case as a street soldier, but some muthafuckas don't get it. That's more of y'all problem than it is mine, so deal with it. If given this chance again, hell yes, I would take it. I may switch up some things that I did, basically, be a li'l bit smarter about some of the choices I made. But all in all, I still would kick Jada's ass again. Ain't no trick gon' put her hands on me and get away with it. Period."

"I know that's right, Prince," Sylvia agreed. "And remember that not all of us judged you, okay?"

Jada threw her hands in the air. "Oh God, there she goes again. Please close your mouth, Sylvia, or go somewhere and change that dress that's showin' too many potholes in yo ass. Prince, you don't like me, I don't like you. Let's be done with it, boo. No love lost here."

"None," Prince said and then looked at Jaylin. "Some of that shit you said to me when I got here stuck with me. When I grow up, I wanna be down like you. I ain't talkin' about all that madness you got goin' on with women, 'cause if they let you do that shit to them, that's on them. Either way, that's yo business, not mine. I'm talkin' 'bout how you do things moneywise, that makes sense to me. I like yo style. If you got some free time in yo schedule to school me on some business tips, I'd be grateful."

Jaylin stood and casually walked over to Prince. He slapped his hand against Prince's and gripped his shoulder.

"I'll make time. I know exactly where you've been; been there too. Keep yo head up, and I'll let you know how to reach me before I leave."

Prince nodded and Jaylin walked back to his seat. Any woman

who didn't appreciate a man like Jaylin didn't understand him. I did. Sylvia was only bitter because she had spent too much time trying to figure him out, rather than trying to figure herself out. That was unfortunate.

We all took deep breaths after Prince had spoken. His words calmed the room, with the exception of Jada who had her lips poked out. Jeff had several index cards in his hand, flipping through them.

"Before I start to ask questions from some of your fans, I would like for Jada to open her gifts. Rush, can you please bring all of the gifts from the table over here?"

Jeff's assistant brought the gifts to Jada, setting them in front of her. She was all smiles while rubbing her hands together.

"Thanks to everyone, with the exception of Jaylin, who brought me a present. I don't know what y'all got me, but I do appreciate y'all's generosity."

The first present Jada opened was from me. It was wrapped in pink paper with a big white bow on top. She looked at me smiling, while pulling the paper away from the box.

"I think I know what this is," she said giddy as ever.

"No, I doubt it. I have a feeling that you're going to be surprised."

She peeked inside of the box. Almost immediately, her face fell flat. She squinted to be sure that she saw exactly what she thought she saw. She then pulled out a jumbo, black dildo with suction. The dildo was nearly twelve inches long and two inches thick. Almost everyone shook their heads, but I thought the gift was appropriate, especially since Jada hadn't lucked up on any dick while she was here.

"Did you mold this mutha off Roc's penis or what? I can't believe you would give me somethin' like this. What was your purpose?"

She didn't seem to appreciate my gift, but I thought it was genuine. I mean, what kind of woman wouldn't appreciate a dick as long as that one? Fake or not, Jada had to give it a try and experiment on it.

"My purpose was so that you could have something to toy with when you get home. I know that being here has made you kind of hot and bothered, but you can work with the dildo in private. We all have to go there sometimes, especially when we find ourselves in a freaky mood, alone or without a man."

Jada held the package and examined it. "This has got to be the most ridiculous gift I've ever gotten. If this package was open, I would knock you upside your head with this rubber dick. I'm not stickin' this mess inside of me. You are wrong to assume that I don't have a man because I do. Just in case you want to know, he was here the other night, screwin' my brains out. So don't get things twisted. If I want some dick, it is well within my reach."

Sylvia reached out for the package. "If you don't want it, I'll take it and put it to good use, especially since all of the men I've been with have fallen short. The last time I checked, man or not, dildos come in handy."

She cut her eyes at Jaylin, but all he did was sigh and shrug. He also ignored our conversation about the dildo.

Jada passed the dildo to Sylvia. Even though I was highly offended, I didn't say a word. She reached down to pick up the next present.

"I hope this one is better. It should be, especially since it's from Roc."

She opened the box that was wrapped in brown, plain paper. When she lifted the box, inside was a hefty bag of marijuana. She snapped her fingers and danced around in her seat.

"See, that's what I'm talkin' about, baby. Roc sholl knows how to treat a woman well. I knew he would come through for me. I wish he was still here, so I could give him a big ol' hug, and a juicy, wet kiss."

Jaylin cleared his throat. "I think you may want to look at your gift again. Better yet, smell it."

I thought I had smelled something horrible, but I figured Jada had passed gas. We both sniffed the air, and when Jada picked up the heavy bag and sniffed it, she threw it on the ground.

"What the fuck is that?" she yelled. "Ugh, that mess smells nasty."

As the glob of whatever laid on the ground in front of us, it was more revealing. It kind of looked like horse manure, mixed with shreds of grass. Jada opened a card that was inside and read it: *The horse shit stinks, just like the mess you created. Fire it up, though, and choke on that shit. Congrats, ma, you've found yourself another enemy. I am who I say I am, and I will do what I say I will do. Kill and destroy.*

As Jada tore up the card, Prince laughed his ass off. Sylvia sat with a twisted face, and all Jaylin did was shake his head.

"That's fucked up," Prince said. "And the funny thing is that shit really looks like weed."

"Then bring yo happy ass over here and start smokin' it. You just as stupid as Roc. Like you, he's been talkin' tough since day one and ain't done nothin'. Both of y'all cowards. He lucky that he got up out of here already."

"Silence yourself, Miss Piggy," Prince said. "Stop makin' that noise and open your next gift. I got you somethin' that I think you gon' like."

She pouted and crossed her arms. "I'm not openin' any more gifts, Mr. Magoo. Jeff, if you would please get this horse shit from in front of me, I would appreciate it."

"Sorry about this," Jeff said. "I thought the gifts would be a nice gesture."

Jeff's assistant and one of the bodyguards quickly removed the horse manure. It stank so badly that everybody winced and frowned.

"Now that the horse manure is gone," Jeff said, "Jada, please open your other gifts. You only have two more of them to open. Then we can move on to more questions."

She sighed and cut her eyes at Jeff. She unwrapped another pretty package. This one was from Sylvia.

"I hope this is somethin' I can use," Jada said and then looked at Sylvia.

"I think you'll be able to use it. Hopefully, quite often."

She opened the box and inside was a Hooked on Phonics box, labeled the premium edition for ages seven to nine. There was also a small dictionary inside of the box. She looked at the dictionary, quickly picked it up, and flung it past me. Luckily, Sylvia ducked. She shot up from her chair and moved toward Jada. Jada jumped from her seat and held up her tightened fist.

"Come on, bitch," she said, rolling her hands in circles. "I've been waitin' to tear that ass up. Just a few more steps and you gon' run right into these knuckles."

I was going to let them fight, but Jaylin stood to intervene. He addressed Sylvia, who was all mouth and no action. She didn't want none of Jada. If she had, she would have moved forward.

"Go take your seat so we can hurry up and get done with this," he said. Sylvia didn't budge. She evil-eyed Jada and stood with her arms folded.

"You'd better listen to the man," Jada said. She drew an imaginary line on the ground, using the cane. "'Cause if you step over this line, yo ass is mine."

Jaylin reached for Sylvia's arm, but she snatched away from him. She pointed her finger close to the tip of his nose. He gazed at her without a blink, as if she had lost her mind.

"Don't touch me ever again," she hissed. "Especially if you don't want to get spit on."

"The day you spit on me will be your last day on earth. I'm trying to save you from getting the shit beat out of you, but at this point, I don't give a damn."

He sat back down and opened the pathway for Jada and Sylvia to clash. Sylvia did exactly what I figured she was going to do—she sat her fake self down.

"Finished?" Jeff said. "I mean, this is so uncalled for. I'm at a loss for words, and I don't quite know what to say."

"I know exactly what to say," Jada said. "Better yet, I know what to do."

Without using the cane, Jada got up and dumped Sylvia's gift in the trash. She returned to her seat and crossed her legs.

"You are so ungrateful," Sylvia said. "I paid almost seventy dollars for that gift. I purchased the premium edition for you, because it appears that's where education started to fail you. I'm sure there were plenty of things you could have learned from that kit, but your loss, Jada, not mine."

Jada stuck up her middle finger and didn't bother to respond to Sylvia. Truthfully, I wanted to see the two of them fight. I disliked Sylvia so much that I wanted Jada to wear her out. I was hoping that Jaylin did something to her too, but he didn't seem like the kind of man who would put his hands on a woman. Then again, if she had spit on him, I wondered what he would have done.

"I guess I may as well open this last gift," Jada said. "No matter what is it, Prince, I swear I'm not gon' argue with you."

Prince shrugged. "That's because you won't have to."

Jada opened the box that had black tape on it. Inside was what looked to be a simple gift card. Jada removed it from the box and read what was on the tiny card.

"Yo cookin' was good, but yo attitude stinks. The gift card is worth fifty dollars. Since you can't buy yourself a new personality, buy some new pots and pans with it. Congrats on yo win. The Almighty Prince aka Street Soldier."

Prince looked away and whistled. Jada was trying to hold back her smile, but when she couldn't, she stood and reached out her arms.

"Aww, give me a hug, boo. Thanks. That was real sweet of you."

As Jada used the cane to limp forward, Prince stood and backed away. "Don't come over here. I appreciate yo cookin', but that's it. Do not touch me, please."

They were being real playful. I thought it was kind of nice of them to make peace with their situation. Thing is, I doubted that it would last for long. And what in the hell was up with Jada and this cane? It was obvious that she was faking like she was hurt. Little did she know, she looked hideous.

She plopped back in her chair and looked at Jaylin. "Jaylin, where my gift at? Why you, of all people, ain't get me nothin'?"

"Because I only buy presents for people who are special to me. That's why."

"So, are you sayin' that I'm not special to you?"

"You're special. Just not special to me."

She licked out her tongue. "Screw you, you curly head, crooked dick fool. Ugh, I swear you get on my doggone nerves with that smart mouth of yours."

To no surprise, he didn't respond. We all looked at Jeff, who sat with the index cards still in his hand.

"Okay, let's move on. I can't ask you guys all of these questions, but I will choose a few. Please answer only if the question is directed to you."

We all agreed.

"Jaylin, you received the majority of the inquiries, along with Roc, but he's not here to answer them. Chase, you were next, so I'll start with Jaylin and then you. Keli from St. Louis believes that Roc has a lot to lose from having sex with Chase. She wants to know, Jaylin, if you regret having sex with Chase or do you think you have anything to lose."

I was a little tense. Jaylin was known for throwing shade and hurting feelings, even if he wasn't trying to. I knew he would be honest in his response, but there was no denying that the truth sometimes hurt.

He held up three fingers and looked at Jeff. "There are only three things in my life that I've ever regretted. One, that I wasn't around to save my mother from being killed; two, that I haven't been able to shake my feelings for a woman I consider a dear friend; and three, that I didn't honor my vows and I fucked over the only woman I have truly ever loved. I regret nothing that has happened between me and Chase, and when I get ready to go there again, I will. I have nothing to lose. Every decision that I make benefits me, and in one way or another, I always gain something from my actions."

I wanted to jump up and down, scream for that matter, because I figured Jaylin was feeling me. His eyes said so. I was so good at reading men. Sylvia and Jada didn't like his response, but too darn bad. I loved it.

"Thank you, Jaylin," Jeff said and then shifted his eyes to me. I was surprised that he was being nice to me. I'd been playing him off since I'd left. I barely answered any of his calls, and I had only answered when I needed him to get certain information to Jada.

"Chase, Chris from Illinois had an interesting question. First, she applauds your scandalous behavior and attitude. She's dying to know your motive and she wants to know why you willingly gave yourself to two men in the house and not to Prince?"

Prince removed his cap and scratched his head. "I was wonderin' the same thing too. Why not, Chase?"

I laughed and answered as best as I could. "No offense to Prince, but I'm only interested in men, not boys. Prince still has some growing up to do, but if I was the same age as him, or close to it, I may have gone that route. While some people make a big deal about sex, I don't. I think when you find yourself attracted to some-one, make sure they're strapped up and go for it. It makes no sense to waste time creating fantasies about men who your heart desires. I like to explore and live out my fantasies. That's exactly what I did. So my motive was to satisfy my desires to the fullest. After that, I checked out of here because I assumed Roc and Jaylin would take issue with my approach to satisfy myself."

"Ladies and gentlemen," Sylvia said. "Those are the true words, spoken from a whore. What a shame. How can anyone admire you?"

I crossed my legs and laughed at Sylvia's comment. "Jealousy will only continue to hurt you, not me. And if you think I care about you calling me a whore, think again. I may even agree with you, but at the end of the day, so-damn-what if I am a whore? I'm good at what I do, and my whore status doesn't allow me to be a scorned woman like you who is mad because you keep running into a brick wall, searching for true love that you'll never find. Wise up, hooker, you're getting too old for me to have to keep schooling you."

She had nothing else to say but "Whatever." I guessed I shut her up, at least until Jeff posed the next question to her.

"Sylvia, Candace from California wants to know why friends don't appear to be off-limits for you? To her, you made a mistake with your best friend's man, and then you turned around and had sex with that man's friend. Are you willing to do brothers?"

"Boom," I said unable to control myself. "Please pick up your face from the ground because Candace just splattered it."

Sylvia put up her hand, ignoring me. "We have no control over who we fall in love with. And if we find ourselves attracted to someone in particular, so be it. I do have limitations, and I would never do anything like knowingly sleep with brothers. What happened between me and Jonathan was an isolated incident that I learned some valuable lessons from. What happened between me and Jaylin was a huge mistake that I regret. But it's not like I can go to him and ask for my goodies back. What's done is done. No one is going to make me feel guilty about my choices."

I didn't bother to offer my feedback. The only reason she regretted being with Jaylin was because she felt dissed. If he would make her an offer to leave right now, she would jump on it. That was why I considered her a phony.

Jada had been kind of quiet. That was a relief to all of us. I hated when Jeff called her out to answer the next question.

"Jada, many of the comments that came in about you were positive. But Bernice from Indiana said she found you to be a bit much. She had hoped that you would be voted out of the house, and she wonders what you believe you contributed to Hell House."

With her mouth dropped open, Jada looked around and then pointed to her chest. "Who me?" she said to Jeff. "You need to recheck those index cards. I can't believe she thought I was a bit much, but nobody else was. Please find out more about who this Bernice person is, because she don't know how to chill out and have fun. Hell House wouldn't have been nothin' without me in it. That's why I'm gon' happily walk my tail up out of here with one hundred thousand dollars. I'm sure she won't be happy about that, but Miss Bernice, do me a favor, please. Mind your business, get you some black dick in your life, then go somewhere and sit down. After that, hopefully your attitude and reception about me will change. Next."

Like a real dummy, the word she was reaching for was perception, not reception. Bernice was on point about Jada, whether she liked it or not. My mouth was covered the whole time she spoke. Prince was shaking his head and so was Sylvia. Jaylin's nonchalant demeanor remained on display, and all Jeff could do was move on to the next question.

"Prince, there's no secret that you were the most disliked person in the house. I guess you rubbed many people the wrong way, but the next question is from Nikki in Atlanta. She says that with all of the fatherless children you have in St. Louis, why not focus more on trying to win this challenge, so you could have money to support your children? She felt as if your effort was lacking and you had more reasons than anyone did to win."

Prince removed his cap and turned it backwards. He leaned forward and clenched his hands together.

"Man, I don't want to hear that noise about how many people couldn't get down with me. If I rubbed them the wrong way by stayin' true to myself, so what. The lady who thinks I got fatherless children runnin' around in St. Louis would be incorrect. There were several chicks who lied to me about those babies bein' mine, and the two kids who are really by me are bein' handled. Maybe I didn't give it my all to win the challenge, but with the women in the house ridin' Roc's and Jaylin's nuts, I was cooked from day one. That was pretty clear, and I was lucky to be in the house for as long as I was. What I'm sayin' is, strategy or no strategy, the women would have voted me out, regardless."

I didn't appreciate Prince's nut-riding comment and neither did Jada or Sylvia. Sylvia spoke up before either of us did.

"I disagree with you for saying I was riding their nuts, because I wasn't," she said. "I don't know where that comment came from, because I treated everyone fairly."

Jada let out a deep sigh and growled. "I hate a trick who suffers from amnesia when somethin' doesn't benefit her. The comment came from his knowledge of knowin' that you rode Jaylin's nuts while you were in that closet. It came from you ridin' his dick in the bathroom the first night you were here and it came from you ridin' Roc and tryin' to get him to notice you. Stop tryin' to act all brand-new, Sylvia, it's irritatin'."

"Exactly," Prince said, cosigning. "I couldn't have said it better."

Sylvia snapped her head from Prince to Jaylin, expecting for him to clear up her dick-riding status.

"Would you refer to my approach as dick-riding?" she said to Jaylin. "I'm curious, because I don't appreciate the bad rap I'm getting. I certainly do not view it that way."

He was straight to the point. "I'm not going to answer your question. We have nothing to say to each other. Direct your question elsewhere."

She folded her arms and lost all control. "Why? Because I told you the truth about yourself and you couldn't handle it? Come on, Jaylin, grow some balls and accept what I said to you like a real man. Don't cry about it. If I touched a nerve, kudos to me. That's one point for me and a big fat zero for you."

Jaylin looked at Prince. "Yeah, she was riding; riding so much that it made me sick. But she did so like an amateur. Had she perfected her dick-riding slash sucking skills, maybe my vote would have swayed in another direction. But, unfortunately, I saw no need to take up extra space in the house with a lame-ass woman who was incapable of making me remember what her pussy felt like five minutes after I jumped out of it." He fixed a stare on Sylvia. "Face the facts, you've been called out. Go fix that pussy and see what you can do to enhance your sexual performance. If you need help finding someone who can teach you, let me know. I know plenty of women I can refer you to. Chase would be one of them."

I turned around in my seat to look in another direction. "Damn" was all I could say. Jada was rocking back in forth in her seat, ready to explode. "Ooooo, this is gettin' real U.G.L.Y. 'cause somebody don't seem to have an alibi. Where in the hell is the popcorn, soda, and Boston Baked Beans? The score is tied. Sylvia, I'm turnin' the mic back over to you. Do your thing, girl, I got my whole dollar on you."

She stood and straightened the wrinkles in her dress. "I'm not going to sit here and let everybody team up on me. First it was the vote, now this."

"Man, ain't nobody teamin' up on you," Price said. "All I stated were the facts, and you don't want to acknowledge the truth. We've all been talked about and called out on our shit. Cool out and chill."

Sylvia ignored him. She stormed toward Jeff. "I'm out of here. I've had enough of this. Do not contact me to do any nonsense like this again. As far as the contract goes, I would appreciate it if you would tear it up. If you have to, sue me."

In a blink, she was gone. I couldn't believe it, but then again, yes, I could. She could dish it out, but wasn't strong enough to take it.

Jeff seemed disgusted. He stood and laid the index cards down in the chair. "I figured this wouldn't be easy, but I appreciate all of you for hanging in there until the end. With Roc and Sylvia gone, we're going to wrap this up. Before I present Jada with the check, I want to thank each and everyone one of you for taking time out of your busy schedules to enter the Hell House challenge. All of you contributed something great to this project, so pat yourselves on the back for giving it your all. Jada, as the winner, I ask that you come forward to receive your check for one hundred thousand dollars. Many feel as though you deserve it. I must say that I agree with them."

Jada blushed as she wobbled to stand on her feet. I clapped and shouted. "Woof, woof."

Jaylin didn't budge and Prince's lips were pursed. As she glided her way up to Jeff like she had just won the Miss America Pageant, she grinned from ear to ear. Then, she squeezed her leg, as if it hurt.

"Ouch. I need to hurry up and get out of here, so I can go see about this leg. It sho' is botherin' me."

Jeff handed her an envelope. When she opened it, her eyes got real big. "OMG," she shouted and touched her chest. "This is really happenin'."

"Speech," I shouted, feeling so good because we had pulled this off. "Let's hear a speech!"

She held her stomach and appeared very excited. So much so, that it looked like she was having an anxiety attack. "Okay. Breathe," she said, taking deep breaths and fanning herself with her hand. "I need to breathe."

She kept joking around. I could tell she was playing, but I was ready to get this done and over with. I was excited about claiming my half of the money, and I wanted to find out what Jaylin was getting into tonight. For whatever reason, Jada was stalling. She'd better not have a heart attack before putting my cash into my hands. After that, I didn't care what happened to her.

"I...I want to thank God for makin' all of this possible," Jada said. "Thank you, Jeff, for comin' to me with this idea, and a special thanks to everybody in the house for puttin' up with me. I had hella fun, but I am so glad to be gettin' out of here, knowin' that I will never have to see any of you mofos again."

I noticed that she looked directly at me. Plus, she didn't single me out to thank me. I had to throw a little something into her thank-you speech.

"Our friendship can't be forgotten," I said. "You may not see anyone else, but you'll definitely see me again."

She winced and put her hand on her hip. "I don't think so. All of my loyal friends live in North County. Some went to Hazelwood East, some Sumner High School. I haven't gained any new friends within the past two years, so I don't know what you're talkin' about with the friend stuff."

"I'm talking about our newly found friendship, where you have my back and I have yours."

I was trying to hint around, without letting anyone know I was talking about the money. She knew darn well what I was talking about. It seemed to me that she was trying to renege.

"Chase, I'll call you in a week or two, so we can talk about that friendship thingy, okay?" She turned to Jeff. "It's urgent that I get to the emergency room to go see about myself. I don't know what's goin' on, but my legs, back, and stomach hurts. I thank you again, and I hope this check don't bounce. If it does, I'm comin' for you."

She tried to rush out of there before clearing up what we had discussed about the money. I hurried out of my seat and called after her.

"What?" she turned around and shouted.

I kept my voice lowered. "You know darn well what. I know you're not trying to skip out of here without saying goodbye, are you?"

I made weird facial gestures, so she'd know what I was referring to.

"Oh, that," she said with fake laughter. "I got you. Just call me in a week or two, girl. I need to quickly call a cab, so I can get to the hospital."

I hated to be played for a fool. At this point, I was so mad about how things were starting to fall apart that I inched closer to Jada and whispered to her through gritted teeth. "If you fucking play me, heifer, I will destroy you. We need to get to the bank first thing in the morning, so that you can give me my half of the freaking money that I earned."

Jada took a few steps back. "All that teeth grittin' mess don't scare me, and just so you know, your breath stank. Name callin' will do you no good either. The more I thought about this, the more I came to the conjunction that I'm not givin' you one damn dime."

The wrinkles on my forehead deepened. "Come again, I didn't hear you. And it's conclusion, you dumb, bitch! I concluded that you will pay up."

Before I knew it, I lifted my hand and slapped the heck out of Jada. I slapped her so hard that the hairs on her head shifted into another style. Before she could lay one finger on me, one of the bodyguards grabbed her. She swung out wildly, but the majority of her punches landed on him.

"Yo ass better run," she shouted. "When I get loose, I'm gon' wear you out."

So much was going on that I hadn't noticed Jaylin and Prince standing near Jeff. Jeff pulled on my arm to move me away from Jada. The other bodyguard had to jump in to restrain her; she carried on like a deranged woman.

"Let me go," she shouted with spit flying from her mouth. She kept swinging the cane, trying to reach me. "I need to beat her ass before I get out of here."

"Ain't nobody going anywhere," Jaylin said, raising his voice. "Calm the hell down, before I have ninety percent of you mutha-fuckas in here arrested."

We all turned our heads to look at Jaylin. He gave Prince a piece of paper and asked him to leave. "You don't have anything to do with this, so take this and get at me tomorrow."

Prince read whatever was on the paper. He smiled and then saluted us on his way out. "Peace to all of you suckers. It's been real."

He jogged away and was now history.

Jaylin looked at the bodyguards. "Let her go, and Jada, go have a seat. That check you have may not bounce, but if you leave out of here with it, I assure you that a stop payment will be placed on it."

The breaking news definitely had my attention. Jada's too. She wiggled her arms, trying to get away from the bodyguards. They refused to let go of her, so Jaylin addressed Jeff.

"Tell them to back the fuck up. Now!"

Jeff appeared nervous. He sighed and told the bodyguards to let Jada go. I was definitely watching my back. I stood close to Jaylin for protection, and since Jada didn't take a seat, neither did I.

Jaylin looked disgusted and quickly spoke up. "Section 565.250 to 257 of Missouri Law refers to the invasion of ones privacy and prohibits anyone from videotaping others without their knowledge, especially in the nude. It is a crime, a felony, that is punishable by law and any person or persons involved can be charged and sentenced up to twenty years in prison. I'm not sure who will be prosecuted first, but I need everybody's full attention. Jeff, you fucked up by allowing a piece of pussy to interfere with a challenge that could've benefited all of us. I have no respect for you, and if I didn't care about sitting in a jail cell tonight, I would bust you upside your head for being so goddamn stupid. To save yourself, get that check from Jada and tear it up. Then pack up your shit and return the ten thousand dollars that I gave you for information about what Jada and Chase were up to. I'll expect that money by tomorrow morning or else you, and any others involved, will have law enforcement knocking at your doors."

Hearing that Jeff had accepted money from Jaylin for information about our plans had my head spinning. I could barely move and neither could Jada. Being in jail for up to twenty years didn't sit well with me. We weren't sure if we were going to jail or not. Jaylin didn't seem to be bullshitting about pressing charges for being illegally taped. How I ever found myself in this mess, I didn't know.

Jeff snickered and tried to throw us under the bus. "Unfortunately, Jaylin, I didn't film anything that showed nudity, nor did I film anything without consent. The only things I filmed was what you and everybody else gave me permission to do. Anything else was done by Chase and Jada without my knowledge. So you see, my hands are clean."

"What the fuck are you talkin' about?" Jada shouted. "I didn't film shit! Yo tail is lyin'!"

"Neither did I," I said, lying through my teeth. I knew Jaylin could tell I wasn't being truthful by the way he looked at me.

Jaylin smirked as he looked at Jeff. "Looks like I have myself a set of witnesses who actually lived in the house and can vouch for who was filming what. You don't have any witnesses, so tear up the check, Jeff, conclude your mission and walk away from this. Unfortunately, none of this will make it to TV unless I say so, and you'll never reap the benefits of the half million you were supposed to get. All contracts need to be null and voided, and we all need termination letters within two days, if possible."

I was so stunned by this. Jeff had this all planned out from the beginning. He was the one who stood to gain the most from Hell House. I didn't say one word. Jaylin seemed to be handling this appropriately and was doing so rather well. Besides, I wasn't sure how much trouble I was in just yet. I guess it served me right for trusting a backstabbing trick like Jada and expecting her to pay up. She was really going to snub me.

Jeff hesitated to make the next move, but eventually, he fell in line. He reached his hand out to Jada. "Give me the check," he said.

She rolled her eyes and slowly walked up to him. With her head hanging low, she removed the check from the envelope and kissed it.

"This is terrible," she said near tears. "I can't believe I let y'all fuck me over like this and get me caught up in this mess. And then to put me in a position to do some jail time wasn't even cool."

Catching Jeff off guard, Jada lifted the cane and started wailing on him with it. "Muthafucka, I told you not to play me," she said with each whack. "Didn't I?"

Jeff crouched down to protect his face. The bodyguards rushed over to grab Jada. One had her by the waist and the other one snatched the cane from her hand. When Jeff lifted his head, his hair was scattered and his shirt was ripped from Jada pulling on it. Jaylin and I had backed away, allowing her room to let out her frustrations.

"Let her go," Jaylin said. "I'm sure y'all can understand how she feels."

The bodyguards let Jada go. Jeff tried to straighten his shirt and gather himself. He touched his bloody lip where Jada had busted him in the mouth with the cane.

"Let's pack up everything and go," Jeff said, wiping his mouth. "We're done here."

"You damn right you are," Jada shouted. "And I'mma report yo ass to the Better Business Bureau."

Of course she didn't know any better, but oh well. Jeff and his crew started to gather their things to go, while Jaylin stood between me and Jada.

"Whatever beef y'all still got, squash it. It ain't worth it, so stop making fools of yourselves, especially over money. I'm not gon' press charges against either of you, but if y'all ever think about selling those videos or pictures, y'all gon' have a big problem on your hands. Now give me some hugs and get out of here. I may have to call the police on these fools, and I don't want y'all around if something pops off."

Looked like my business here was done, but I still had further business to tend to with Roc and Desa Rae. I was on edge about the money that I was supposed to get, but was glad that Jada would leave here without one single penny. She reached out to hug Jaylin before I did.

"Thank you," she said with her head buried against his chest. "I should've known better, but like you said, money is the root of all evil. There was surely some evil and connivin' people around here. I sholl wish I had some of that money, though, and is there any way possible that you'll consider hookin' me up on the side like you promised to do?"

Her words shocked me. I couldn't believe that she tried to cut a side deal with Jaylin. And then she had the nerve to talk about somebody being conniving.

"Not a chance in hell," he said. "You fucked up. Just be thankful that you won't be going to jail."

She backed away from him with sadness in her eyes. "But I had plans for that money, Jaylin. I wanted to get myself out of debt and take a trip with two of my girlfriends. You can give me some-thin', can't you?"

"I'm giving you a lot. Your freedom. Now, stop being ungrateful, go pack your bags, and take your stride up out of this house like all of us have had to do."

She lowered her head in a playful manner and walked off singing Carol Burnett's theme, "I'm so glad we had this time togetherrr, just to have a laugh or sing a soooong…"

I couldn't help but laugh to myself. She was a damn fool. Once she was out of sight, I reached out to hug Jaylin. His body felt solid as a rock, and the smell of Clive Christian was tickling my nose. He smelled so spectacular that I didn't want to depart from him. I was surprised when he lowered his hand to my ass, giving it a light squeeze.

"You looking good, baby," he said. "If I didn't already have plans tonight, it would be on."

I pulled my head back to look into his eyes. "Plans to do what?" I asked.

"That ain't your business."

"Maybe not, but is there any chance of you canceling your plans?"

"I could, but I don't want to. Now, go on and get out of here. I'm staying behind for a minute to make sure there won't be any bullshit with Jeff."

"Okay, but promise that you'll call me. Soon. I left a couple of messages on your cell phone, but you've been ignoring me."

"Been busy. And I don't make promises I'm not sure I can keep."

He was playing hard to get, but for the hell of it, I stood on the tips of my toes, removed my arms from around his waist and let them fall on his shoulders. I leaned in for a kiss, indulging myself as I sucked his tongue into my mouth like it was a dick. His hands roamed my backside and he squeezed in the right places. I could feel the growth of his muscle right at my midsection. The more it grew, the further he moved away and licked my wetness from his lips.

"Goodbye, Chase," he said with a memorable, sexy smile on his face. "Stay sweet for me."

"You bet I will."

I winked at him and decided to leave it there. I removed my arms from his shoulders and sauntered away. Jeff could barely look my way, but when I caught his eye, he turned to look in another direction. That was fine with me. I was glad to be leaving Hell House for the second time, on my way to bigger and better things with my sister, Ms. Desa Rae Jenkins.

Jaylin

The day was long; too long, and I had other things to do. Jada had packed up her things, and she asked if I would help her carry her bags to the taxi. I did. Once her stuff was placed on the back seat, she got inside to sit down. She left one foot on the ground, while leaving the door opened. Her mouth widened, but before she could say a word, I spoke up.

"Six people divided by one hundred thousand dollars is approximately sixteen thousand, six hundred and sixty-six dollars. That's all I'm giving you because you did not play fair, plus, you fucked me over."

She opened her mouth wide, showing her off-white teeth. "I'm sorry. I won't do it again, but are you for real? You gon' give me some money? Was that my gift?"

"Yes. If I said I would give you the money, then I'm gon' do it. Now, make this quick and tear one of your checks out of your checkbook and give it to me."

She cocked her head back and her face fell flat. "A check? What for?"

"So I can deposit the money into your account tomorrow."

"Aw, but, uh, do I look like I got a checkbook affiliated with me? I was gon' take the check Jeff gave me to his bank or to a cash-check place around the corner from my house. I'm in Telecheck. These folks out here don't trust me with no checks. Hard times, baby, real hard times. You wouldn't know nothin' about that, though."

I released a sigh, hoping she was playing. I had a feeling she wasn't. "You need to get yourself together, ya feel me?"

"I will, and if you round that sixteen up to twenty thousand, it may help me get a bit more stable faster. As far as the money goes, what about a Visa Green Dot card or my RushCard? Can you put the money on there?"

"Never heard of a Visa Green Dot or a RushCard. I've got plenty of Visas, so I don't think you know what you're talking about."

She shook her head. "Jaylin, Jaylin, Jaylin. Your wealth has you so out of touch. I understand that you don't have to use prepaid cards, but you should at least know what they are."

"Yeah, whatever. I'll do twenty g's, but give me your phone number so I can contact you tomorrow with a new checking account number. The money will be in there, so make smart choices, invest, and spend it wisely."

Jada had no idea that I was really going to deposit fifty grand into her account. I had my reasons for doing so. I removed my cell phone from my pocket and held it. She was giddy as ever. Tears filled her eyes as she reached out to grab my neck, holding it tight.

"I'm so grateful right now. Damn it, Jaylin. Not only do you have a big dick, but you got a big heart to back it up. I understand why so many women love you. You the bomb, baby. So fuckin' real, I swear."

I liked doing nice things for people, especially for women who had a certain impact on me. But I wasn't down with all this mushy shit, so I gave Jada a pat on the back and then backed away from her. She provided me with her phone number, and after putting her leg into the taxi, I closed the door. I watched as the taxi took off and was out of my sight. I had no regrets hooking up Jada, and I intended to hook up Prince too. They were young people who I thought needed an opportunity. Everybody else in Hell House, they were on their own.

With the premises being clear, it was time to get down to the real business. I made my way back into the house and onto the patio where Jeff and a few of his crew remained. Jeff was sitting in a lounging chair with his feet propped on the table. I pulled back on a chair and sat across from him. We stared at each other and then smiled.

"Section 565.250 and twenty years in prison, my ass," he said. "You are so freaking good, man, I swear you missed your calling as an actor. I wasn't so sure if you could pull this off."

"Neither was I. When Jada started kicking your ass, I thought you was gon' say fuck it."

"Not a chance in hell, even though she banged me up pretty good."

We laughed and agreed. Jeff placed the contract on the table for me to sign it. It was a 2.5 million dollar contract that paid me as the creator of Hell House. I sold it to the network who was the highest bidder. They knew it would be a hit like I did. The only thing that I asked to be excluded was Roc's sexual escapade with Chase. Everything else was a go. Jeff would get his cut as the executive producer and the participants in the house had a chance to become famous. Plenty of opportunities would come knocking at their doors, but it was up to them to pursue opportunities that increased their financial statuses. My deal here was done. Business prospects for me were endless. I had figured out another way to line my pockets with money without anyone knowing that I was behind this. Not even my best friend, Shane, knew. I kept telling him that I was a real winner. Maybe in due time, people would start to believe it.

Jeff and I shook hands on our deal. I had to meet with someone else, so I jetted. On my way out the front door, I dialed out on my cell phone to make sure he was going to meet me at the restaurant at ten. With the phone close to my ear, I headed to my Midnight Blue Aston Martin that was parked several feet away from the house. As I got closer, I squinted and saw Chase sitting on the hood of my car. It was pretty dark outside, and the only light came from a streetlight that was near the corner. Her backside on my hood was a no-no, so I clicked the end button on my phone and put it into my pocket. The frown on my face let her know that I didn't approve of her ass being on my car.

"Don't look so mean," she said as I walked up to her. "Smile. I'm sure somebody loves you."

"Get off my car. Your heels may scratch it and I don't want any dents in it."

She eased off my car, stood, and folded her arms. "Sorry, but I thought I'd wait until you were finished. I don't know what took you so long, and I thought Jeff and his crew had roughed you up in there. In five more minutes, I was going to bust in with my shotgun."

"Good thing you didn't have to. I had to put closure to that shit, and I'm glad it's a wrap."

"So am I. But I seriously hope that you're not going to put closure to us. It would be a shame for the two of us to go our separate ways after this. Don't you think so?"

"It doesn't matter what I think, especially since I have to be some-where important in like," I lifted my wrist to look at my Rolex, "like in forty minutes."

Chase reached out to pull on my belt, bringing me forward. "Whoever she is, she can wait. I, on the other hand, can't."

She unhooked my belt buckle and pulled my shirt outside of my pants. I loved spontaneous sex with beautiful women, so I didn't dare stop Chase. She unbuttoned the buttons on my shirt and then rubbed her hands on my carved chest. I inched forward, but she lightly pushed me backward, causing me to stumble a little.

"You know you're out of control, don't you?" I said.

"I do. Therefore, I need a man like you to tame me and take control."

Her eyes gazed into mine, as she hiked up her dress and exposed her shaved pussy that waited for me to fill it. Not from the front, but from the back. Chase turned on her stomach and poured her body over the smooth curves in my car. She stretched her legs far apart, and I'd be lying if I said the position she had on my car wasn't a beautiful sight. Having my full attention, she reached her hand back to smack her pretty ass. It jiggled, causing my dick to rise to the occasion and signal for an exit. I reached in my suit jacket to retrieve a condom. After tearing the package open with my teeth, I slipped it on. I moved forward, and not wasting another minute, I leaned in and positioned Chase to receive every inch of me. The moment I rotated my hips, a loud moan escaped from her mouth that remained open. I stirred her pussy juices, even while my cell phone rang. I knew it was Roc by the ringtone, but I wasn't about to exit no pussy that was this sopping wet. Roc and I had to reschedule. As a potential future business partner, he'd understand that there were times when some things came before business.

When I discovered how the women in the house tried to play Roc, I had Jeff reach out to him. And even though Roc had backstabbed me, I didn't want to see him caught up in no shit with the woman he loved. I'd been there too. I only wished that somebody had saved my ass. But either way, I met with him while he was at the hotel. We discussed how to bring Hell House to closure. I explained everything to him, and when I offered to give him a substantial amount of the money I'd made, he shocked me when he refused to take it. All he wanted was possession of the pictures and for his sexual encounter with Chase to be erased from the film. In addition to that, he wanted peace. I told him that I would use everything within my *power* to get Chase to back off, but we knew that she was a force to be reckoned with. Roc agreed that if all efforts had failed, he would deal with her in his own way. He was appreciative of me for reaching out to him and we discussed other things to partner up on to make money.

We even discussed Sylvia, who had left on a fucked-up note. Some people couldn't be saved; I definitely wasn't trying to save everybody. She had some things she needed to work on, and even though she talked a good game about reevaluating herself, there was no action. The same applied to Chase. All she was good for was sex. No man would ever take her seriously until she got real with herself, got to the core of her problems with men, and dealt with it. Until then, she would continue to put herself out there like this.

I heard a thump that knocked me out of my thoughts. My suit jacket and silk shirt were now hanging off my broad shoulders. I had kicked up a sweat trying to milk all that I could from Chase's pussy. The way she was working me, though, I was sure she had dented my car. She stretched her arms wide and squeezed her fists. Another moan followed as my fingers circled her swollen, tension-packed pearl. She moistened her lips with the tip of her tongue and released a soft moan.

"Mmmm, this dick is…it's spectacular, Jaylin. I sooo wish you were on the receiving end of this, just so you could have a better understanding of how the way you're sliding that thing in and out of me feels."

Her wetness soaked the condom. While holding her waistline, I kept grinding my steel to reach the depths of her tunnel. "I'll take your word for it, baby. I know how you feel. I'm also confident that you wouldn't lie to me about my performance."

Chase kept backing it up and I kept hitting that pussy in the right spot, causing it to show out for me. Before entering Hell House, I hadn't indulged myself like this in quite some time. Considering all that had happened in my life lately, it's been all work, not much time for play. I couldn't help but to think about Scorpio believing that I couldn't get hard anymore. I had to laugh, as the old me would've called her and put Chase on the phone so she could give Scorpio explicit details about how I was making her feel right now. I could only imagine what would happen if the two of them ever came in contact. They had a lot in common, and the hell from this house would revert to hell in my house. The more I thought about it, though, Naughty is what I had perfected. And there was no secret that scandalous men always appreciated scandalous women. Chase was messy too, but if anyone could *tame* her, bring her back to reality, it was definitely me.

On the verge of an explosive orgasm, Chase pulled her cheeks further apart, allowing me to have the best view of the night, while watching my rhythmic insertions. Her pussy was stuffed, and as her creamy glaze started to cover me, she turned her head to the side and closed her watery eyes.

"You're there," she cried out. "Right where I…I need you to tickle that spot and fuck me harder. Go hard, baby! Turn this shit up and dig deeper into this pussy. It's talking to you, Jaylin. Don't you hear it speaking?"

"Loud and clear. Keep talking."

To avoid her cum from flowing on the hood of my car, I grabbed her hips and pulled her to me. I positioned her pretty ass right in front of me, and honored her request to turn this shit up. Chase's pussy kept talking. Talked so much that, after her orgasm, she faced me and threw her arms tightly around my neck. I caressed her trembling body, keeping it close to mine. I could feel her heart beating fast, and as we stood in silence, I chuckled at the thought of her being in my Naughty clique. Shame on me for daring to go there, but a man like me would never let a pussy that speaks so clearly to me pass me by.

"What are you thinking about?" Chase whispered. "You've been awfully quiet."

"Just thinking about how good you were to me and about how we all won this challenge without even knowing it."

Chase cocked her head back to look at me. "Winners? Really? My pussy may be a real winner, but my pockets are still empty. And I'm not sure if the others would agree with you on the winning thing or not."

"Maybe, maybe not. But when you have an open mind, you'll see what I mean."

She shrugged and straightened her clothes. I watched Chase, thinking about her comment. In my opinion, she was the sex-game winner. From day one, it was her motive, and she had conquered all. If she was disappointed about not being a big winner, maybe she should have set her stakes higher. Prince was the life-lessons winner. He gained much knowledge, hopefully making him a better young man. Roc won pertaining to relationships. When you know better, you do better. I predict that after his woes are worked through, he'd be on the right path. Sylvia got another wake-up call about self and friends, and Jada could possibly be the biggest winner of us all. Hell House put us in a position to prosper, but prospering wasn't always about money. It was unfortunate that Chase wasn't smart enough to realize it, so with that in mind, I washed my hands of her. Good pussy with the lack of brains didn't do much for me these days, so I said my goodbyes, got in my car, and jetted.

Surprised? Don't be. It's how I, Jaylin Jerome Rogers, smoothly operated. Hate me or love me, I represent who I say I am. I pressed my foot on the accelerator, zooming in and out of traffic while thinking about the future of Hell House. The thoughts of it made a smile wash across my face, and I winked ahead at what all of this would eventually lead to.

Two words: Stay tuned.

ABOUT THE AUTHOR

A St. Louis native, Brenda Hampton is recognized as being a writer who brings the heat. She has written over twenty-plus novels, including anthologies, and her literary career is filled with many accomplishments. Her name has graced the *Essence* magazine bestsellers list, and she was named a favorite female fiction writer in *Upscale* magazine. Her mystery novel, *The Dirty Truth*, was nominated for an African American Literary Award, and she was awarded, by Infini Promotions, for being the best female writer.

Hampton's dedication to her career, and her original literary works, led to a multibook deal. She works as a literary representative for an array of talented authors, and she is the executive producer of an upcoming reality TV show, based out of St. Louis, Missouri where she resides.

In an effort to show appreciation to her colleagues in literature, Hampton created The Brenda Hampton Honorary Literacy Award and Scholarship Fund. The award not only celebrates writers, but it also represents unique individuals who put forth every effort to uphold the standards of African-American literature. Visit the author at www.brendamhampton.com and www.hellhouse.homestead.com